THE
ANASTASIA
CONNECTION

IN THE CAROLYN ARCHER MYSTERY SERIES

Millicent

The Anastasia Connection

THE
ANASTASIA
CONNECTION

Veronica Ross

A *Midnight Original* MURDER MYSTERY

THE MERCURY PRESS

The publisher gratefully acknowledges the financial assistance of the Canada Council and the Ontario Arts Council.

AUTHOR'S ACKNOWLEDGEMENTS
The author wishes to thank the Ontario Arts Council for assistance.

Cover illustration by Todd Mulligan
Edited by Beverley Daurio
Cover design by Orange Griffin
Composition and page design by TASK

Printed and bound in Canada by Metropole Litho
Printed on acid-free paper
First Edition
1 2 3 4 5 00 99 98 97 96

Canadian Cataloguing in Publication Data
Ross, Veronica
The Anastasia connection
ISBN 1-55128-038-8
I. Title
PS8585.O842A63 1996   C813'.54   C96-931711-5
PR9199.3.R67A63 1996

The Mercury Press
137 Birmingham Street
Stratford, Ontario
Canada   N5A 2T1

For Sarai

Chapter One

Saturday, 7:00 a.m.: Conrad was just starting his throwing-up-wood routine. "Ah-haah, ah-haah." Heave, heave. Peter's head snapped up from the pillow. "Geez, not on the bed, Conrad! Get off the bed!"

The phone rang. It was Marion, my mother-in-law.

"Carolyn! Did you watch the news last night?"

"No, we were out late... Hold on a sec."

"Go on!" I pushed our four-month-old yellow Labrador Retriever to the bottom of the bed. Peter opened an eye and groaned.

"Sorry, Marion. Conrad took off for the woodlot last night and dined on wood out at Emma and Mark's. He's in wood pulp production again." I nudged Conrad's splayed hind legs with my foot. He grinned and lunged towards me. I hastily stuck my free hand under the covers, and he made for my chin. "No! Bad dog! No nipping! No!"

"Sorry," I told Marion, shoving Conrad away.

"I shouldn't have called so early," Marion's fine English voice said as I wrestled Conrad onto his back with one hand.

"What about the news?" I asked.

"The duplicate DNA tests on the tissue sample from Anna Anderson proved she really wasn't the Grand Duchess Anastasia. She was that Polish peasant Franziska Schanzkowska after all, the deranged factory worker her enemies said she was. I was hoping the first tests had been a mistake, but the other tests confirmed she was Schanzkowska!"

"What, I— " Conrad pulled free and bit my arm. "No, Conrad. No!" I grasped him by the scruff of the neck as we'd been taught in Puppy Kindergarten.

"I don't believe it, I just don't believe it!" Marion went on. "The ears matched and the handwriting expert who authenticated Anne Frank's diary said Anna Anderson was Anastasia. Do you think they could have tampered with both results, or switched both samples? But I don't see how one could switch a piece of someone's intestine! There was a program on Nova about the tests this week, but I missed it!"

Conrad bit Peter's nose.

"I'd better call you back later or your son will be minus a nose," I told Marion.

Or we'll be minus a dog, I thought, as Peter yelled and swung his legs over the side of the bed.

I made coffee and sliced bread for toast while Peter-of-the-nicked-nose took Conrad for his morning walk. Instead of a leash, he tied one end of a Venetian blind cord to Conrad's collar and the other end to his belt, the idea being that the dog should follow the master, not vice versa. Conrad's trainer at Puppy Kindergarten swore it would work. We'd purchased the cord on our way to Emma and Mark's last night.

While the coffee perked I got out the clippings Marion had sent me. I had read the clippings, and also the books Marion recommended on Anna Anderson, but mainly out of politeness. I had never been convinced that Anna Anderson was Anastasia. And I didn't want to get involved in another royalty story.

Marion found the mystery of Anastasia engrossing. Peter said she was obsessed by it; obsessed by royalty, period. There was a time when I had been similarly obsessed. After my friend, Millicent Mulvey, died— she claimed she'd been married to Edward VIII— I have to admit that I read every royalty book going (while my brain slowly turned to mush) in an attempt to find out the truth about her claim.

Afterwards, I swore I'd never touch any royalty subject again. And it is— I know it is— intellectually suspect to show an interest in royalty. I mean, what intelligent person could evince the slightest concern about Diana and Charles and all the rest of them, especially after all their problems and fights were public knowledge?

I knew exactly why Marion had called. A few years before, her cousin Ethelina had been visiting from England, and we all went to Oktoberfest in Kitchener to suffer from polka music. Hank from Illinois soon swept Ethelina to the dance floor, and Marion chatted about the latest Anastasia book. She had to almost yell to make herself heard, and a man sitting next to us overheard and told us he'd lived near Anna Anderson in Hanover, Germany. When Marion told him about my cookbooks and mysteries, he wanted me to write a book about Anastasia's lost fortune. No government in the world, he claimed, would permit a publisher to bring out this book about the Tsar's hidden wealth. We'd have to finance it ourselves.

I got a headache just thinking about the beer we consumed that night (except for Peter, the designated driver, who grew grimmer by the minute). There was a lot of talk about Anna Anderson's shelves full of books (books in many languages, all hidden by a curtain), about how she'd taught this man sitting next to us to ride a bike, and how he'd had the run of her apartment as a boy.

The man's name was George Austin-Wright. German mother, English father, he said, which led to a boozy vilification of the father, who'd absconded years ago, leaving little George— pronounced the German way: Gay-org— in Hanover.

With beery wisdom and insight, I said: "Are you sure you're not related to Anastasia? You look exactly like Nicholas II!"

He did, too— at least in the low lights of the dining room of the Concordia Club with the beams and stucco walls and beer steins, plates of bratwurst, waitresses in dirndls, *Lederhosen* on the waiters, and polka music punctuated by toasts. "*Eins, zwei, drei, Zuffa!*" and down the hatch went the beer.

George Austin-Wright, aka Nicholas II, burst into tears. Peter poked me in the ribs.

I had been supposed to meet the Tsar's look-alike the next week for coffee, but I never kept the appointment.

Over the years, Marion remarked wistfully from time to time that she wished I'd seen Mr. Austin-Wright again. And now she'll want me to find him, I thought, staring at Marion's clipping about the discovery of the bones of the Tsar's family in the woods near Ekaterinburg, Siberia, where the family had been imprisoned. They'd found the bodies of everyone but the youngest daughter, Anastasia, and the hemophiliac heir to the throne, Alexei.

The Tsarina, Alexandra, elegant, cool, distant, be-jewelled, unhappy, looked back at me from a photograph in another clipping. The devotee of Rasputin. The granddaughter of Queen Victoria. One of the richest women in the world. Gossip about her involvement with Rasputin had fanned hatred for the imperial family. Alexandra urged Nicholas not to grant a constitutional government. Rasputin proposed ministerial appointments to Alexandra, who in turn pestered the Tsar into acquiescence.

"How would you act if you were Anastasia and no one recognized you?" Marion once asked me. "Imagine surviving the massacre and escaping to Romania and trying to commit suicide in Berlin in 1920. And then her own relatives wouldn't accept her, even with the forensic evidence!"

Another reason I was always sceptical of Anna Anderson's claim was because she "refused" to speak Russian, saying it was the last language she'd heard when her family was killed. Her story of escaping to Romania, where she married her rescuer and had a son, lacked proof. Anastasia's favourite aunt, the Grand Duchess Olga, who had known her very well as a child, denounced Anna, as did other close relatives.

And yet, she had her supporters, including cousins of the real Anastasia, and the court trials about her identity lasted almost forty years.

I stared at the picture of Franziska, the "demented Polish factory worker." It was a dim, blurry picture, taken in the country, beside what looked like a hay stack. Franziska wore an apron and a necklace looped over a bow-tie collar.

She did resemble Anna Anderson, particularly around the mouth. And the look in the eyes was similar— a secretive, amused, distant look.

Last year, when the first DNA tests, done in England, claimed the tissue sample matched the Schanzkowska DNA, Marion had remained sure that further DNA tests would prove Anna Anderson was really Anastasia. I'd put her off looking for Mr. Austin-Wright, saying we'd better wait for the test results to be confirmed. Now she would want me to find him, and it would be difficult to refuse.

Peter burst through the door, a torn piece of Venetian blind cord dangling from his belt.

"I don't believe it! I just do not believe it! The little devil gave one big pull and off he went!"

I threw on jeans and joined Peter in the hunt for our miniature serial killer. We're not polished suburbia in downtown Guelph, and there are no immaculate lawns. But the old limestone and brick houses do have rock gardens and hedges. Conrad had dug holes in two rock gardens and watered most of the hedges. He had demolished one be-ribboned corn husk broom, and he had run into the open door of old Mrs. Hunter's house while she was hosting a recital for her piano students.

Luckily we found Conrad right away at the bottom of Lancaster, but it took half an hour of chasing and calling before we cornered the grinning, tail-wagging mutt under a Lincoln Continental parked at the other end of the street.

Peter was half an hour late opening The Bookworm in downtown Guelph.

Marion wasn't at home when I called at ten. She was at the library, my father-in-law Hugh informed me testily.

Hugh used to be the Police Chief in Meredith. After his retirement, and after a long-awaited trip back home to England, he and Marion had turned their house into a Bed & Breakfast. Hugh saw his role at The Meredith Inn as the hearty English host in the manner of the noble lord who's turned his feudal estate into a tourist establishment, but Marion became much spunkier once she started earning money, and Hugh, alas, often found himself clearing the breakfast dishes, making beds, and even cooking.

Fall wasn't their busy season, and they were planning to close in November, but they had two American deer hunters in residence. I pictured Hugh with an apron wrapped around his girth while he scraped dishes.

"She must be looking up something about Anastasia." I imagined Marion, right after breakfast, airily scooting off in her new (to her) yellow bug.

Hugh snorted. "I have always known that Anderson woman wasn't Anastasia. It's a complete waste of time."

Hugh and Peter rarely agreed about anything, yet they had both been appalled by Marion's and my involvement with Millicent's story. But while Peter thought the very idea of royalty was nonsense, Hugh was all for Queen-and-Country.

"I always maintained she was the Polish woman," Hugh proclaimed. "If she had been Anastasia, her relatives would have acknowledged her."

I heard a dish smash.

"Oh, bloody hell!"

"Did I hear something break?"

"No, it was the clock ticking."

"Talk to you later. Can you please tell Marion I called?"

"If I'm here. I am apparently supposed to transport the grandkids to visit their father after I finish scullery duty."

Peter's sister, Allison, had recently kicked her husband Joe out.

Joe moved in with his mother, and Allison was refusing to deliver the children to their father for weekend visits.

"Well, tell Marion when you can. What's the latest on the Allison front?"

"War," Hugh said. "She won't have him back. I'll be transporting the kids until I'm old and grey."

"You're old and grey now."

"Bloody hell."

"How's Joe?"

"Suitably contrite. Otherwise he's the same blockhead he always has been. They will no doubt reconcile, but in the meantime I'm the one who drives the youngsters and listens to old Joe's mother caterwauling that Allison has been just like a daughter to her. Joe promises to quit drinking, which will make him all the more unbearable."

"Leave Marion a note if you're going out."

"I imagine she'll get back to you as soon as she returns from the library. How's the mutt?"

"Blessedly, suspiciously quiet. Sleeping on the couch the last time I saw him."

"He's a hunting dog," Hugh said with disapproval. "You're asking for trouble using a working dog for a lap dog."

Before Hugh hung up, he said Marion would undoubtedly get back to me the minute she flew in. No one in Meredith, he said, wanted to discuss the Anastasia nonsense with her.

When I got off the phone, Conrad was chewing the corner of our new handcrafted, braided rug. We'd had it made in the summer in blue and apple green with bits of coral to liven it up, and now a patch was unravelling at the outer edge. Conrad grinned at me and dashed right over.

"What am I going to do with you?"

I grabbed him and held his nose to the tear and went through the "No! No!" routine. We'd have to shift the whole rug, turn it around so that the rip would be under the couch. The ugly blue comforter from Zellers which we'd bought to cover the couch was already torn. We'd removed the patchwork throw cushions and we'd even moved a wall hanging from Peru a few inches higher above the couch.

"They say go for the dog who comes to you," Peter had said the day we went to pick out our dog. He had fond memories of old Chip, his boyhood dog, a "bloody mongrel" as Hugh described him. Now Conrad, named after a character in Peter's one and only unpublished novel, was to replace Chip. I hadn't really wanted a dog, having been bitten as a child by a crazy German Shepherd who lived down the road from my grandmother's house in Maine, but Peter had been hoping for a dog for a long time.

Naturally, "Conrad" had to be a male. There were only two males left in the litter when we arrived. The lighter one ran to hide beneath the raised dog house in the kennel, but the larger, deeper yellow one bounded over to Peter and began scrambling up his legs.

I fell in love the minute the furry bundle nestled in my arms and stared at me with his brown eyes. With all his faults, Conrad had quickly become the focal point of our lives. "I wanted a dog and we had to end up with Conrad!" Peter would say with despair and pride.

I called Peter at The Bookworm.

"Guess what Conrad's done now?"

"Don't tell me. What?"

"He chewed the rug."

"Christ. Now that's ruined."

"No, we'll just turn it around. Shift the furniture."

"Where were you?"

"Talking to your father. Your mother's at the library, probably looking for recent newspaper articles about Anastasia. I can't watch Conrad all the time."

"What did you do to Conrad?" Peter asked suspiciously.

"Told him he was bad. Don't worry, I didn't hit him."

Hitting was a no-no, according to the oracles at Puppy Kindergarten. But I'd been tempted, more than once.

It was noon before Marion called back. She had read a British newspaper at the library. Not only did the second intestine tissue sample match the Schanzkowska DNA, but a hair sample test performed in the United States had had the same result.

She wanted me to find George. It shouldn't be hard, she insisted. He owned a nursery between Kitchener and Guelph.

"Hugh says I'm mad. If you find this George I might even come to Guelph to talk to him myself. If it's convenient, that is."

"It's always convenient. You know that. Anyway, I'm between books, kind of at a loss." I had started a new mystery about a woman being stalked, but it seemed to be going nowhere.

"I still think the DNA business could be a frame-up. Just find out if this George fellow's still around. You don't have to get involved, Carolyn."

"If I do find him, he might not want to see me. I did stand him up. He struck me as terribly officious, not to say nuts."

"Why, because he kissed your hand?"

"He did?" I didn't remember that.

"He did. He also told you were beautiful and much too young-looking to be an author. He said you looked about eighteen."

"Hmm." I did remember something about that. Because I'm small, with frizzy dark hair— and I'd worn jeans that night— people often think I'm a teenager, but only from a distance. "He must have been pretty loaded. And he hinted he was Anastasia's son! I mean

Anna Anderson's son. Remember how he wept? I don't imagine he'd want to be her son if she was only a Polish peasant."

"I just want to talk to him."

"All right, I'll try to find him. Hugh will be thrilled if you come to Guelph now."

"The devil take him," Marion said.

"I think she was really the Schanzkowska woman, Marion."

"They said she would never be recognized, even after her death."

It didn't take me long to find George Austin-Wright. The name was the clue: Old Hanover Nurseries— not very original, considering his background— on a back road between Guelph and Kitchener. I knew the place; it wasn't far from Scottie McGrath's farm, where we'd bought Conrad.

Chapter Two

I had to take Conrad with me; I couldn't leave him at home by himself. Scottie had advised us to purchase a crate, translate cage, which he assured us would be Conrad's own sweet home, but the idea of imprisoning our pup had seemed monstrous. Now we were sorry we hadn't followed Scottie's advice. Leaving Conrad loose in the house was like leaving a maniac on the rampage— good-bye shoes, slippers, table legs and any paperbacks lying around (he'd chewed up Grass' *Dog Years*, the brilliant thing) and the few times we locked him in the bathroom he not only howled piteously, but ate the toilet paper and mangled the bath mat.

Luckily, he was content to sit in a stopped car, regarding it as his den. Driving with him was another story. Usually, one of us held him while the other drove. I could have waited for Sunday, when The Bookworm was closed and Peter was off, but I didn't want to suffer the harangues I'd experienced from Peter when I was tracking down Millicent's story.

"We're going out to your old stomping grounds," I told Conrad, putting him in the back seat of our new Volvo (purchased from the combined royalties of my last cookbook, *Keeping the Harvest,* and my new mystery, *Murder in the Kitchen*) along with Squeaky, the green rubber fish Conrad slept with. "Be good or I'll drop you off there."

The backroads between Kitchener and Guelph are real country, seemingly a million miles from the plazas and malls that make up so much of southern Ontario's countryside. Small farms and stone houses predominate. People from all over the world have settled in the cities, but the rural area is still populated largely by descendants of the pioneers who came from England, Scotland and Germany to break up the forests and till the land. Some of the farmhouses are almost stately, but others are like country houses everywhere: little bungalows with sagging roofs and wood piles, miscellaneous vehicles in the yard. Now that it was fall, the fields were stripped and bare. The post-harvest time always made me wish for snow and look forward to Christmas, to the thought of bright lights and families gathered around the fire.

The brilliant red of the trees relieved the drabness, however. I found myself thinking of another fall day in October when Peter and I had toured the countryside looking for pictures of pumpkin fields for the cover of my cookbook, *Winter Ovens.* We had eaten at the Stone Crock, a Mennonite restaurant near Kitchener, and later I'd broken into Millicent Mulvey's house.

How angry Peter had been!

"Back! Get in the back seat!" I yelled at Conrad, who was

jumping to the front. Next he'd pull my hand away from the steering wheel. I reached into my pocket and threw a dog cookie over the seat. He scrambled back. Crunch, crunch.

"Want to visit Scottie?"

It was the wrong thing to say. Anything was the wrong thing to say, because Conrad took my voice as an invitation to invade the front of the car again. I threw another cookie to him.

Conrad started barking madly as soon as we turned down Scottie's lane, but I doubted if he remembered the place. He'd been only six weeks old, almost too young to leave his mother, but Scottie said Baby, the bitch, had weaned her puppies.

Conrad must have smelled the dogs. Scottie had both Baby and General, Conrad's parents, out in the yard.

"Scottie" was apt, because he was from Scotland. His real name was Humphrey. "Scottie" came from the guys at the union hall. Scottie was an electrician. Forty-something, short, thin and wiry, he had the kind of blonde looks that reminded me of either an old man or a teenaged boy. He was unmarried. He and his mother Mabel had emigrated together, and Mabel looked after the kennel by herself—when Scottie worked.

"So how is the chappie?" Scottie asked through my rolled-down window. I held Conrad firmly in my arms, but he twisted and pulled to be free. Baby and General sat obediently at heel, although Baby raised her muzzle and sniffed at the car.

"As you can see, we have him enrolled in Puppy Kindergarten."

Scottie reached out a freckled hand to touch Conrad, who growled at him.

"He's very protective of the car I'm afraid."

"You don't want him to be letting every Tom, Dick and Harry into the car now, do you?" Scottie pulled his hand back and regarded Conrad. "Bonny he is, and strong."

"He's still nipping."

"They'll do that until their second teeth come in. You can stop it, though. Let's have a look."

As soon as I opened the door Conrad scurried over my lap and yipped at his parents, who remained at heel. I hurried out with the lead, but Conrad was away, circling the larger dogs, barking and wagging.

Mabel came out of the farmhouse with a basket of laundry. Thin and blonde like her son, she always looked like she'd been scrubbing floors. She wore an ancient housedress and a brown sweater. Only she would hang laundry out in the nippy October air, I thought. Behind her was Lady, her mongrel sheep dog. But even Lady trotted obediently beside Mabel when she walked over to inspect Conrad.

Conrad attacked Mabel's wicker clothes basket.

"Tut, tut." Conrad stopped and looked at Mabel, who swept the basket up out of his reach.

"Lively little wire," Scottie commented.

"Down, down," Mabel said in an off-hand way, brushing Conrad away from her legs and setting the basket on the porch steps. The steps were new, installed since the last time I had been out here. Their house was large, with a porch running along the front and large maple trees providing shade in the summer. The place would have been handsome had it not been covered with ugly, imitation red brick siding made of tar paper. But Scottie and Mabel were gradually fixing it up.

We shook hands. Mabel's were red and chapped and I smelled bleach as she knelt down to pat Conrad, who sat perfectly still while she talked to him in a soothing voice.

"We must be doing something wrong," I said.

"You must have confidence," Mabel said, getting to her feet. "He's a lovely little dog."

"We hope having him neutered will help," I said. The McGraths nodded. We'd gotten Conrad at a discount, since, in Scottie's opinion, Conrad's legs were a bit long for the breed and he wouldn't, therefore, be a good candidate for stud.

"Play," Scottie commanded his dogs, and with leaps, Conrad's parents took off for the field with their son after them.

"You can go, too," Mabel told Lady, who was off in a dash.

"How about putting the kettle on, Mother?" Scottie asked Mabel. "I'll keep an eye out for Conrad," he told me.

"Watch that Conrad doesn't get any wood. It's his food of choice these days," I told Scottie.

Mabel's kitchen was plain, clean, utilitarian. Only the geraniums blooming on the windowsill and a rocking chair with a black cat dozing on it livened up the room with its fifties red arborite table and white appliances. There were no fridge magnets, no newspapers lying around or dishes sitting in the sink.

But there was something about Mabel McGrath I liked. Seemingly so charmless, she was also frank and honest. Plain spoken. When I mentioned I was going to the Old Hanover Nursery, she wasted no time in telling me what she thought.

"We have nothing to do with them. They have the most terrible dog, a wicked and unruly Alsatian who bit Lady once. We've had words with them about Hans— that's the Alsatian's name, if you can imagine it.You want to watch yourself when you go there."

"I was bitten by a German Shepherd as a child."

"They generally keep Hans chained up, which is half the trouble, if you ask me. There's nothing wrong with Alsatians, nothing wrong with the breed, but every once in a while you get a strange one."

"You get strange people, too," I ventured.

"And none stranger than them down the road. The only time the older gentleman talked to us was when we had words about Hans, and the words were not very pleasant. His name's English, but he's German. Acts like the Gestapo."

"Who else is there?"

"The son, Johnny. He's friendlier than the father, but something of a layabout. Father and son don't get along, I hear. It's only a small business they have."

"Was Lady bitten badly?"

"Eight stitches in the shoulder. We had to take her to the veterinary emergency hospital, and they charge a small fortune."

"You could have taken them to court for the costs, at least."

Mabel shook her head and hugged her thin elbows.

"It would only have been an aggravation. And Lady was loose. She ran away occasionally in her youth."

"I met the father once, at Oktoberfest in Kitchener. He knew that woman who said she was Anastasia. They lived near her in Hanover."

I looked at Mabel to see if she knew the story. She did, and remarked that the woman had died in the States, hadn't she?

"Yes, in 1984, I believe. Mr. Austin-Wright claims she taught him how to ride a bicycle, of all things. Anyway, my mother-in-law wanted me to track him down. She's interested in Anastasia."

"We saw a show about the DNA tests on television. I was not surprised she was not Anastasia. Royalty can tell their own."

"I thought your neighbour looked an awful lot like Nicholas II."

"That is because you were at Oktoberfest," Mabel said drily, "although the airs that man assumes always put me in mind of King Midas!"

The Old Hanover Nursery seemed a poor setting for King Midas, or an illegitimate scion of Tsar Nicholas II.

A rusty white van sat in the driveway. It was a small place, a clapboard house with an office downstairs and a greenhouse around the back. I don't know much about gardening but it seemed to me that the apple trees to one side of the drive needed pruning, and the house definitely could have used a coat of paint.

Conrad was tired after his run and he made only a half-hearted attempt to escape from the car when I opened the door, but he came to with frantic yipping when he heard the German Shepherd's mad barking. The beast— Hans— was chained to a dog house beside the greenhouse. The chain looked sturdy, but it rattled and clanged as the dog pulled and snarled. He was huge, at least a hundred pounds, and his fangs were enormous. He seemed to be foaming at the mouth.

I ignored Hans— he *was* tied up— and made my way over a flagstone path to the office. The door was open, but no one was there. I could have walked off with the few dusty boxes of tulip and daffodil bulbs displayed on the counter beside a box of gardening gloves. Only a giant healthy green elephant plant and several lush spider plants hanging from the ceiling advertised that this place belonged to people who grew things. Sacks of fertilizer and bone meal lay in the corner.

I dinged the bell on the counter. The MasterCard sticker was peeling off.

"Hello? Hello? Anyone there?"

At last I heard footsteps. A young man with long blonde hair in a pony tail came from somewhere in the back. Johnny, the son, I thought; the owner, no doubt, of the rusty van. I couldn't imagine Nicholas II's look-alike driving such a decrepit car.

"I was just driving by and I noticed your sign and thought I'd pick up some bulbs."

"Not many left, I'm afraid." The voice was pleasant, polite. Johnny smiled at me and moved a box over.

"Quiet time of year." I made conversation as I selected two boxes of red bulbs and fished out my credit card.

"But soon we'll be into the Christmas cheer," Johnny said happily. "We sell a lot of Christmas trees."

"I'll have to remember that."

"Get them shipped from Nova Scotia."

"You know, I think I may have met your father once. George Austin-Wright. I think he said his nursery was around here."

Johnny stopped writing and looked at me. For a moment, he seemed cross, but he averted his face as he ran my card through the machine.

"I think it was at the Concordia Club, at Oktoberfest."

"He's been known to go there," Johnny said. He shrugged, obviously not thinking much of Oktoberfest. "But he missed it this year. It's the last night tonight."

"Really. I didn't know that. But we don't see the Kitchener newspaper. I always hoped I'd meet him again."

Johnny raised an eyebrow.

"Oh, this is nuts," I said. "I didn't really come here to buy bulbs— no, I'll still take them, you don't have to tear the slip up, I can always stick them in the ground. I came here specifically to talk to your father. It was just a chance meeting at Oktoberfest. I went because a relative from England wanted to go and your father overheard my mother-in-law mention Anastasia, that woman Anna Anderson— "

Johnny laughed.

"You know what I'm talking about? I'm a writer and your father wanted me to write about her."

"Me, too," Johnny said.

"You're a writer too?"

"No, no. I write some poetry, but nothing really." He waved his hand dismissively. But mention writing to someone who writes "some poetry" and he has to ask, "What do you write?" which he did, and I told him.

"My father wanted me to write about Anastasia, too."

"But you wouldn't."

"Cor-rect. You got it. I told him to write it himself, but apparently he wants a front of some kind because he knew her."

"The DNA tests proved it wasn't her anyway. Two or three separate tests."

"Who cares? Maybe I've just heard too much about it. My father gets these ideas, these crazy schemes."

"I'm actually looking him up for my mother-in-law, who's an Anastasia fan. She still thinks that woman was Anastasia."

"So you want to talk to my father?"

"Is he home? I didn't think he'd be here. There was just the van."

"He doesn't have a car at the moment. Lost his license. Breathalyser."

So you have to drive him everywhere, I thought.

"Come on, then," Johnny said. "I can't call him because he's listening to opera with the headphones on. Wagner. I can't stand Wagner."

I followed Johnny up a narrow staircase. Through a side door I noticed a messy bedroom with books and clothes on the floor, obviously Johnny's.

"Here you go." Johnny swung the door at the top of the landing open, revealing his father, dwarfed by gigantic earphones, reclining in a leather rocker. He didn't immediately notice us. His eyes were closed and his elevated feet, in brown plaid slippers, moved to the rhythm of the music.

He did look like Nicholas II. I hadn't been that drunk at Oktoberfest. His features, although rapt by Wagner, wore that distant regality I'd seen in photos of the Tsar. It was a narrow face, small, with a fine structure.

But then he opened his eyes and saw us. For a moment he glared at Johnny, peered at me, and then he removed the earphones. The music coming through the earpieces was splitting— I couldn't place which opera. He got to his feet.

"Someone to see you," Johnny said.

"Carolyn Archer. You might not remember me. We met at Oktoberfest a few years ago."

I extended my hand, and he indicated with a nod that Johnny should depart. The door closed. George unplugged the earphones and for a minute Wagner's chords thundered through the room. Then, mercifully, he turned the volume down.

The blue eyes were Nicholas' and the expression in them was very much like the expression in pictures of the Tsar. George's eyes were surrounded by dark circles. Anna Anderson's supporters had always said her remarkable eyes were exactly like those of the Tsar. Nicholas' mistress from before his marriage had met Anna Anderson as an old woman and claimed that when she looked into Anna's eyes, she recognized the eyes of the Tsar.

"We talked about Anastasia," I said. "You wanted me to write a book about Anastasia based on information you had. We were supposed to meet, but I was called out of town," I lied, "and I didn't know how to reach you."

"You have found me now," he said stiffly. He had a bit of an accent, but his command of English was excellent. He'd come to Canada in the early sixties, he'd said.

"My mother-in-law recalled you had a nursery."

"Please sit." He indicated the couch. "It is unfortunate your mother-in-law did not know this years ago."

Nice guy, I thought, putting me on the spot. He stood looking at me in a distant and reserved way. I said nothing, like a guilty schoolchild. After a moment, he offered coffee and left the room to prepare it.

If downstairs was grubby, upstairs was a miniature old-fashioned Europa. A heavy wall unit covered one wall. Crystal glasses, leather books, a Royal Doulton figurine and small woodcarvings filled the shelves. The coffee table was high, in the German tradition, and covered with a lace cloth. A series of woodcuts of medieval scenes hung over the couch, and on opposite sides of the window were old paintings of forests and mountains.

"Do you recognize the music?" he asked, returning with a tray. I shook my head. Tannhauser, he informed me, turning the volume up. Magnificent, he said, no? The story of—

The coffee was strong, brewed, not instant. He'd even heated the milk and arranged chocolate biscuits on a plate.

I asked if he'd heard about the Franziska Schanzkowska DNA tests. There was no television in the room.

"Who?" So he hadn't heard.

"Franziska Schanzkowska, a girl from Pomerania. Her enemies in the twenties said Anna Anderson was really Franziska Schanzkowska, a girl who worked in a munitions factory and was injured when a grenade exploded. She was supposed to be insane. I think a detective found Franziska's family in the nineteen-twenties."

"I don't know anything about that," George said.

"It was in all the books about her. Anna Anderson had to meet Franziska's landlady's daughter, who identified her as Franziska. Anna also had to meet Felix Schanzkowski, Franziska's brother. At first he said she was his sister, but he changed his mind when the lawyer asked him to sign an affidavit."

"I have never bothered with those books. Pff. Whatever they wrote about her were lies. They were all only interested in the Tsar's money. They will never allow the DNA tests to show she was Anastasia. Never in a million years! Her enemies would never permit her to be recognized! So you have come to argue with me."

"No, I— "

"She was Anastasia. I can prove it. This book must be written, especially now. I will tell them about the DNA and what they have done to her name! To her honour and dignity!"

"I have newspaper clippings. Maybe you should read them."

"They can write what they want in newspapers."

"But if you want to write a book, you should read all the material on the subject you can.

"I'm only speaking as a writer," I added, when he didn't respond.

"The books do not interest me. They have nothing to do with the real person. The real person was Anastasia, the woman I knew."

"The woman who taught you how to ride a bicycle," I said. "The woman who yelled at you in Russian."

"I see you remember."

"Oktoberfest wasn't a good place to talk, but I remember that you said she had a large painting of Rasputin in her apartment. The eyes followed you everywhere, you told me."

"It's a miracle how she got it out of Russia."

"But she was supposed to have escaped in a peasant cart, after the slaughter of her family. She couldn't have taken a painting of any kind with her.

"That's what all the books said, that this peasant, Tchaikovsky, rescued her and brought her out of Russia to Romania."

George shrugged and got up, taking a key out of his pocket and unlocking a section of the wall unit to reveal a row of bottles. He turned the stereo off. He returned to the table with a bottle of schnapps and two glasses.

"She herself claimed this Tchaikovsky rescued her," I pointed out as he handed me a glass.

He raised his drink in a toast. I drank; it was horribly bitter.

"The gardener's son helped her," he said at last. "Everyone else cared only for the money but the son of the gardener helped her."

"Do you mean the doctor's son, Gleb Botkin? His father died with the Romanovs. They found his body, too. You did hear about the Russians locating the bodies of everyone except Anastasia and Alexei? No one knows what happened to Alexei, either."

He frowned into his glass. The gardener's son? I wondered. What had I heard about a gardener? There was something... I remembered something about a gardener somewhere in this story.

The door opened.

"I need change," Johnny said.

"Again?"

Johnny shrugged. His father gave him a cold look, grumbled something under his breath, and left the room. Johnny grinned at me and spread his hands in a gesture that said, What can I do?

"And I don't want any funny business," his father said to him, giving him a handful of bills. He made a face at the closed door.

"You and your son run the nursery together?"

"He has no interest in anything. I have to keep after him."

"He seemed pleasant enough to me."

"Pleasant, pleasant. So— are you interested in this book?"

I took a breath. "What I'd like to do is to get you and my mother-in-law together. She's read far more than I have about Anastasia. You met her at Oktoberfest, Mrs. Hall. Marion."

"You, personally, are not interested, then?"

"I didn't say that." The man was beginning to annoy me. "There'd be a lot to discuss."

"What is there to discuss? I tell you the information and you write. That is all. No one knows what I know and the rest does not matter. There's no one left from Hanover who knew her well, or in the Black Forest where she later lived, and where we visited her after the war. Perhaps only my mother knows, and her opinion is the same as mine."

"Your mother."

"Tetta Schwartz. She lives in Kitchener."

"She has a different name."

"She married again. She is widowed now."

"What I don't understand," I said, "is why you don't simply write the book yourself."

"Because I will be killed," he said very seriously, and then he did look exactly like Nicholas II. Did he remember crying at Oktoberfest? I wondered. He'd had quite a lot to drink himself that night.

His voice rose. He would give every cent he had, sell his business and the very chair he was sitting in to finance the book! His son would be on the street, but perhaps then the boy would pull up his socks! There was no more honour in the world. George came from honourable people, noble people, and his honesty and integrity were on the line!

I finally escaped, but only after agreeing to an appointment Wednesday night at 7:30, at his house, with Marion.

"So how was it?" Johnny asked me when I came downstairs.

Suddenly Wagner's music thundered down the stairs.

We looked at each other and laughed.

Chapter Three

Peter clutched Conrad in the back of the car on our way to Puppy Kindergarten.

"Do you think he'll ever grow up?" Peter asked.

"Probably not."

"If only he'd stop nipping."

"Sometimes I think we should just whack him."

"We agreed not to do that."

"It's just so tempting sometimes," I said. "People used to hit their dogs with slippers and newspapers."

"Beating kids used to be okay, too," Peter said, as Conrad slipped from his arms and made for the front seat. Peter jerked him back. We already had the lead attached to the choker, not just because Betty the trainer said we could give him a good "pop" if he misbehaved in the car, but also because it was impossible to fasten the leash once we were at the arena.

"Don't tell me you weren't tempted," I said, "when he bit your nose." You could still see the narrow scab where Conrad had nipped Peter's nose.

"To tell you the truth," Peter said, "I don't think he'd even feel it."

With a wiggle, Conrad appeared between the two front seats. Peter gave a pop with the leash, almost strangling him, but Conrad forged ahead. So help me, his tail wagged even while he made retching sounds.

"Don't pop that way!" I cried. "Jerk up, not down!"

"Get back here!" Peter yelled, letting go of the lead and trying to grip Conrad's middle. Conrad jumped on my shoulders. Peter "popped" to no effect and finally hauled him back physically.

"Maybe he'll be better after he's neutered," Peter said.

Conrad started to bay, cry, sing and what I can only describe as "mewl" as soon as we drove through the chain fence of the old arena. He jumped up on the back window ledge and threw himself against the glass.

We had a routine. I got out and Peter gripped Conrad until I opened his door. Then it was holding on, flying after Conrad. Peter's thin legs flailed, his hair stuck out, his glasses slipped as he tried to control Conrad.

Fate awaited Conrad, however. Ninety-pound Betty, Conrad's trainer and personal Hitler, stood at the door. Conrad braked to a stop, sending Peter against the door. Betty steadied Peter with one arm and with the other relieved him of the leash.

She knew how to "pop." Conrad went flying through the air and then he trotted obediently at her side to the ring, where she relinquished the leash to Peter. Conrad's sister, Kelly, was already there with Emma. Usually, her son Thomas had Kelly in the ring.

Conrad attempted an incestuous hump, but a warning "No!" from Betty brought him back to heel.

I joined Emma's husband Mark in the bleachers. Mark said Thomas was at home with a cold.

Conrad behaved beautifully.

Afterwards, we went to Tim Horton's for coffee and to compare dog horror stories. Both dogs, tired from their studies, slept peacefully in their own cars.

I've known Mark and Emma since I came to Guelph in the early seventies. Mark and my first husband, Charlie, were at the University of Guelph together. Mark was Charlie's hippie friend, and lived in a commune outside Guelph. Emma was his lady, and the only permanent woman resident. She baked bread and washed clothes on a scrub board. They had the proverbial goat and sold apples from their orchard. Emma baked pies for the market. Marijuana grew among the corn and peas. All the guys were going to be musicians.

Emma left the commune about the time Charlie and I separated. Mark was stoned all the time and they had a dopey-marijuana argument about the politics of acquiring a washing machine, but the breaking point came when Mark took his clothes home to be washed by his mother, Emma having declined to use the scrub board except for her batik blouses and jeans.

I remember this silly situation well, because Emma came to stay with me when she left Mark. She'd dropped out of university and for a while supported herself waitressing. Her family were fundamentalists from Holland who'd given up on her for living in sin with Mark, but finally she moved back home and later returned to Holland where she trained as a legal secretary.

She came back to Guelph years later with her five-year-old son, Thomas. She was divorced and found work at a small law firm. Mark was a lawyer by this time. One day Emma turned up at court to deliver some papers and there was Mark. Like the song says: "...across a crowded room..."

Mark was engaged (to another lawyer; Emma gleefully reports that this lawyer said, "You're leaving me for a *secretary*?"), but within a week he and Emma were back together. I was a witness at their wedding a month later.

Now they live on a hobby farm near Eden Mills. They've been married four years and Mark has adopted Thomas. We joke that we are related through our dogs. They saw Conrad, fell in love (especially Thomas) and drove straight out to Scottie's that afternoon and bought Kelly.

After the dog talk was exhausted— no, it wasn't exhausted; dog talk was never exhausted— I interrupted a story about Kelly crawling under the car and getting oil all over her and told Emma that Marion was arriving the next day.

"Better your mother-in-law than mine," Emma said, wrinkling her nose and brushing her blonde bangs back. She always reminds me of a picture in a Hans Brinker book I had as a kid. "I haven't seen Her Highness for three weeks. She was going to visit Sunday, but she was afraid of Thomas' germs. I wish Her Highness were more like Marion."

Mark looked uncomfortable. His mother still lunched with the lawyer ex-fiancee. The Richmans were an old Guelph family, active in the Conservative party. Mark's father had been a lawyer, too.

"Speaking of Her Highness, let me tell you why Marion's coming," I said, steering the topic away from Mark's mother.

"Here goes," Peter said, rolling his eyes. "Your mother might be a germ fanatic— "

"— she doesn't like Thomas," Emma interjected.

"— but mine's royalty mad. Insane with it. I feel like stuffing my ears with cotton whenever she's around," he exaggerated. "She's getting kookier all the time. Now she's all worked up about this Anastasia business, and she's going to visit Nicholas II's son."

I began to explain about the deranged factory worker, DNA tests and George Austin-Wright, but Mark cut me off. If dog talk was a late fascination, anything about Russia was an old obsession. Mark might be a lawyer today, but back in the commune days he was a fervent Communist, and even talked about emigrating to Russia. I've often thought that Mark looks Russian, with mad, curly black hair, worn, still today, too long.

"It's just another example of capitalistic greed," Mark said of the Anastasia business. "The parasitic monarchists, the de-throned royals, wanted to get their hands on the Tsar's fortune. Whether there actually was money is another matter. There was Tsarist gold but that belonged to the state, to Russia. Maybe the Romanovs even hoped to get their hands on that. Have you ever seen pictures of the Youssupov palace? The prince who killed Rasputin? Rooms and rooms filled with paintings, da Vinci, Michelangelo, you name it, they had it— bought because they exploited their peasants. So all these grandees are working as chauffeurs and gigolos on the Riviera and along comes this woman who says she's Anastasia. Bingo. Of course they hate her."

"She was really Franziska Schanzkowska, the girl from Pomerania. But she fooled them until she died. Her own lawyer," I told Mark, "an American called Fallows, spent all his own money trying to prove her case. He even sold his house. They said she could never be a Polish peasant, but she clearly was."

"Peasant, peasant," Mark said. "Do you see what I mean? The word becomes derogatory, synonymous with murderer and criminal. Good for Franziska, if she fooled them. She was probably working for the Bolsheviks."

"She hated them," I said.

"Listen to her," Peter said. "I'll have two royalty-mad women on my hands tomorrow."

"The queen in Holland is like everyone else," Emma said. "If you meet her you can talk to her like any other human being."

"Beatrix is one of the wealthiest women in the world," Mark told her. "I bet that this Franziska worked for the Bolsheviks. She was probably laughing up her sleeve at the monarchists."

"She was afraid the Bolsheviks would kill her," I said.

"Oh, I saw that movie with Ingrid Bergman," Emma remembered.

"In the movie, Anastasia was reunited with her grandmother, but in real life her grandmother would never meet her," I explained.

"Don't you mean," Mark asked, "that the Dowager Empress of Russia, Her Imperial Highness the Empress Marie, would not meet Franziska Schanzkowska?"

"What's this 'Dowager Empress' stuff?" Peter cried. "You're all mad. Imperial Highness! I'm the only sane one here!"

Chapter Four

I was raking leaves, and Conrad, tied to the maple tree so he would not escape through a gap in the side hedge and leave a smelly package on elderly Mrs. Pilgrim's lawn next door, was snoozing when Marion arrived in her yellow Volkswagen beetle.

Conrad woke up right away.

"Someone's glad to see you!"

They say the English are dog mad and Marion made as much of a fuss of Conrad as if he'd been a child. She'd had her hair cut and dyed a light shade of auburn. That was a first. I'd never seen her in jeans before, either. Only the bulky Icelandic sweater was familiar. I remembered her knitting it in Meredith the previous Christmas.

"And someone's got a present," she laughed, bending down to rub Conrad's ears. "Mum's got you shackled up, has she? We'll soon fix that." She unsnapped the collar from the chain and scooped him up before he could get away. Not that he seemed to want to escape. He was busy licking her face. "I told you he'd improve, Carolyn. You little dear," she crooned at Conrad.

I hoped she hadn't bought yet another expensive rawhide bone. Ten dollars worth of rawhide meant no more than five minutes' chewing and swallowing to Conrad. "So that's the limo," I said, lifting her bag out of the car while she cradled Conrad, who wasn't nipping at all.

"They also had a convertible but I thought it might be a bit much," she said wistfully. "A white convertible."

Her suitcase weighed a ton. Books, Marion explained. Anastasia books.

Conrad's present was a red and green striped dog sweater.

"Peter will have a fit," I said, as she tried to get the sweater over Conrad's head.

"I had some ends of wool and as soon as I saw the pattern I couldn't resist making it." She thrust Conrad's front legs through the openings and set him on the floor. "It won't even fit him very long, the rate the scamp's growing."

Conrad stared at his legs.

"Isn't he a pet?" Marion asked.

"You look great, too. What's with the hair?"

"If Hugh can dye his hair, I can too!"

"Hugh dyed his hair?"

"Grecian Formula. Suddenly he wasn't grey any more. Can you believe it? I looked like his mother. Look at Conrad, Carolyn."

Conrad tugged at the leg ribbing of his new homemade sweater.

"No, no, don't tear your lovely sweater." Marion reached for him and pulled him on to her lap. "Carolyn, there's a camera in my suitcase. Let me get a picture of him to show the kids. They are dying to see Conrad, by the way."

"Tell Allison to visit," I said without conviction, as I left to find the camera. Peter's sister had only visited us twice in Guelph, both times with Joe, whose idea of a good time was to open a two-four and watch hockey. But even the thought of Allison on her own wasn't appealing. She and Peter had nothing in common and her main interest when she came "south" was hitting the malls.

Marion's little Instamatic was right on top of the Anastasia books— the biography by Peter Kurth, another one by someone called Lovell which I had never heard of, and two books on the Romanovs.

"You hold him while I take the picture. I want the grandkids to see how he's grown."

"This is ridiculous," I said, balancing Conrad on my knees and trying to keep his teeth away from the sweater. "One more, in case the first one doesn't come out," Marion pleaded. "Hugh says we treat Conrad like a poodle. I brought all my Romanov books, by the way. I suppose you noticed."

"There's one I haven't read yet."

"Oh, I know. I keyed in 'Anastasia' at the library in North Bay and found this new book. After I read it I ordered my own copy from Toronto."

"Can I take the sweater off now? I can't hold him much longer."

"Here, let me." I handed Conrad over. "The book's much the same as the others, except it's apparently an authorized biography. Anna Anderson told this fellow she and her sisters survived and went to Perm, another town in Siberia, which was also in that book *The File on the Tsar. And* he claims there was perhaps another sister,

Alexandra, who was spirited away from the palace because she wasn't a boy."

"That's crazy."

"Rumour had it in Russia that Alexandra had a false pregnancy, but this Dutch woman claimed she was a child from that time and that the faith healer who'd promised Alexandra a son smuggled her out of Russia." She wrenched the coat off Conrad, who barked at her.

"That's the nuttiest thing I ever heard. How could anyone smuggle a royal baby out of a palace? With all the guards and valets and footmen? And if Anna Anderson told this writer she and her sisters went to Perm, she had to be lying. The Russians found the bodies."

"I know, I know," Marion sighed. "But I keep thinking the handwriting analysis matched and forensic scientists said her ears were the same. There just has to be a mistake somewhere, Carolyn."

After a late lunch, Marion wanted to show Peter Conrad and his sweater and her car ("just like a teenager!") so we drove to The Bookworm, where Peter was busy arranging new autumn books in the window. He'd recently rented the space next door and the dividing wall had been torn down, making a larger space. I was still undecided about the roomier store. People could browse more comfortably, and it was airier, but that old look of books crowding the shelves had been replaced by something resembling a mall store.

Cass, Peter's assistant for years and years, had surprised us by getting married and moving to Vancouver, and he had hired two part-time clerks to replace her: Lucy, a teenager in Grade Twelve who came in on Friday nights and Saturdays, and Muriel Wilson, an ex-teacher, whom Peter regretted hiring from the day she started. Not only did she attempt to censor the books on the shelf ("I didn't think you'd want this out, Mr. Hall,") but she made Peter feel like a schoolboy, advising him how to arrange the window, for instance, which was what she was doing when we arrived.

"I really don't think the poetry books are a wise choice for the window," she complained to me. "They're simply not going to attract customers."

She was a mousey woman, with wan hair pulled into a tight knot, and she always wore polyester dresses or pants in some shade of beige. I think this very mousiness and the fact that she had worked in circulation at the library convinced Peter she'd be "bookish." He'd been hesitant about hiring Lucy, with her black stockings and shorn hair, but it was Muriel who turned into the headache. The fact that she was recently widowed and supporting a grown-up son (who frequently came in for a hand-out) made it hard to fire her, Peter said.

"Oh, I don't know. A lot of our customers look for that sort of thing," I said. Thanks to Cass, The Bookworm had achieved a reputation for stocking poetry books, and people came from all over southern Ontario to buy them.

I hadn't introduced Marion yet and Muriel pretended she didn't see her. That was another thing. She was awkward with customers. We'd seen the business grow enough to justify the extra space, but if our old customers kept away because of Muriel, Peter would have to do something. ("Shoot her," he suggested.)

"Muriel, I'd like you to meet Peter's mother, Marion."

Muriel nodded and half-heartedly shook hands. "But not the right kind of customers, I told Peter. Those types just come in to look. We want people who buy. We've got those lovely big books on interior decorating and I know we'd sell more if we only advertised them better."

Peter climbed out of the window and kissed Marion's cheek.

Muriel sighed and walked toward the back of the store.

"So you've got the love bug," Peter said, looking through the window. "And I see you brought the pooper along. You'll get dog hair all over your seats."

Conrad, recognizing the store, was scrabbling at Marion's car window.

"There won't be so very much hair," Marion said, "because Conrad's wearing his coat."

"His what?"

"Your mother made Conrad a sweater," I told him. "Come and see."

"A sweater? He's growing a double coat for winter!"

"Oh, it's just a joke, Peter. Come for a drive. Do you have time for coffee?"

"I thought you'd be chasing Anastasia down by now," Peter said, as Muriel approached with a big book.

"It wouldn't hurt to try this in the window," she said. "We can always take it out again. What do *you* think?" she asked me.

"I don't want *Decorating With Your Microwave* in the window," Peter said.

"But we want to sell them! The new poetry books never went out at the library. No one ever checked them out!"

Peter closed his eyes.

"It wouldn't hurt to try," Muriel persisted.

Peter didn't answer, but went to the office to get his coat.

"When I get back she'll have that damn book in the window," he said as soon as we were out of the store.

"Oh, what's the difference?" Marion murmured. "I can't see the harm in her suggestion. She might even have a point."

"The point is I can't stand the woman." He opened the car door and sweater-clad Conrad came flying out. "And I happen to be the boss," he added, trying to hold on to Conrad, who pulled to the fire hydrant.

"He looks like an absolute idiot in that outfit," he laughed.

"Something between Charles Manson and a transvestite. Now go bite that bad, bad Muriel," he told Conrad, whose ears perked, listening. "Bad Muriel, get her! Sic!"

Conrad took off, Peter flying behind. Maybe Peter was Muriel's boss, but he certainly wasn't Conrad's.

Conrad stayed behind with Peter when Marion and I went to see George that night.

"I hope this won't turn out to be a complicated Millicent story," I said as she drove through the darkening Ontario landscape. "I don't think I'd be up to it."

"I just want to talk to this man."

"He'll want you to write a book for him."

"Perhaps I shall."

"You seem pretty confident."

"I am. You are perfectly right. All those years, reading books and knitting sweaters and Hugh being the big Police Chief. Then there was Millicent, and I began to think: This woman lived in the shadows all her life, and why should I do the same? But it was going to England that really made the difference, I suppose. All our relatives and old friends seemed positively decrepit. Stuck in a rut, as they say. Hugh lorded it over everyone, but what had I done?"

"You look ten years younger with your hair like that."

"I feel twenty years younger."

"Well, if you're that interested in Anastasia, go for it. That's what I always tell kids when I do a workshop." After I started publishing mysteries, the schools began calling me to conduct writing workshops. "Whatever you have a passion for, I say."

"And however crazy this George sounds, he has a passion for this story. And that's why I want to talk to him."

"We're almost there. Conrad was born around here, by the way.

The place is just down the road, but we probably don't have time to drop by for you to see the holy of holies."

As it turned out, Marion did get to meet Mabel, who was walking along the dark road. She waved for us to stop. Lady was loose, she said; we hadn't seen her, had we?

"She hasn't disappeared for years. I'm worried she'll get hit by a car. Humphrey'd take the truck to look for her, but he's at a union meeting. I've been calling and calling, but there's no sign of her. She always comes when I call."

We hadn't seen Mabel's dog, but I offered to drive her around to look for Lady. "We're on our way to visit your favourite neighbour, but we can be a few minutes late. Maybe Lady wandered over to the nursery."

Mabel shook her head. "You'll be having quite the welcoming committee, I'd say," she told us. "I went as far as the lane, and Hans was setting off an awful caterwauling. Johnny's van wasn't there and I wasn't staying around to speak to the old man. Lady wouldn't be there anyway, with Hans at home."

She hugged her elbows. No, she wouldn't trouble us. She'd go on home, she said, and wait for Humphrey and they'd go in the truck to look for Lady if "Her Ladyship" hadn't meandered home by then.

With a dismissive nod, Mabel turned on her heel and set off down the road.

"I'm glad Mabel didn't want us to go looking for her dog," Marion said. "I'd have hated to be late."

"Oh, Mabel's independent. Those Scots. Millicent was like that, too. Here we are— you can turn here. I wish the dog wasn't in the house. Hans'll sense I'm afraid."

Lights were on upstairs and the office was lit up, too. Mabel was right about the welcoming committee. We could hear Hans barking even before we got out of the car.

"I don't like this," I told Marion.

"But surely he'll lock the dog up."

"I bet he thinks Hans is wonderful and the beast will lie there and glower and growl the whole time we're here. At least Conrad's friendly. He might be a nuisance, but he thinks visitors come just to see him.

"When I was here on Saturday Hans was chained up outside," I added as we climbed the steps to the office.

My hand didn't even reach the office doorknob before Hans' fangs snapped at the glass. I stepped back, and the movement sent Hans' huge body hurtling against the door.

I rang the doorbell, but this only made Hans more frantic.

"He has to hear that dog barking," I told Marion.

"Maybe the dog has rabies," Marion suggested.

"I'm not about to find out. I say we go to Mabel's and phone. Maybe George has got his earphones on. On Saturday he was listening to Wagner through headphones."

"But then he wouldn't hear the telephone either," Marion protested.

"We can always come back. I don't think he has a busy social calendar."

"Why don't we just sit in the car," Marion suggested. "He's bound to hear the dog sooner or later."

She reached for the doorbell to try again. The door shook in its frame. "Let's get out of here," I told Marion, but undaunted, she shook a fist at the dog and yelled.

Hans backed off and Marion pressed her face close to the glass.

She tottered back as Hans made a lunge for the door.

Marion gasped.

"Mr. Austin-Wright has a hole between his eyes. He's lying at the back of the store and he's— dead."

Mabel telephoned the Ontario Provincial Police. A terrible

business, she said grimly. Terrible. We sat at her arborite table, Marion and I still in our coats. Marion kept repeating that she didn't know how any intruder could have gotten past the dog.

"If that dog hadn't been there..." Marion said.

"You could not be expected to tangle with the dog," Mabel said. Lady hadn't come home and Humphrey was still out. Baby and General had woofed at our arrival and Mabel had shut them up in another room. The kitchen seemed very cold, and I could hear the humming of the red electric clock on the wall. 8:20. Our appointment had been for eight and we'd been a few minutes early, but delayed by meeting Mabel, we must have arrived right on the dot of eight.

Marion's eyes met mine. What if George Austin-Wright had been killed so he couldn't talk to us? At the same time I thought of Johnny and hoped he wasn't involved in a father-son altercation that had gotten out of hand: threats made, the wrong word spoken, the last, unbearable insult. I'd liked Johnny. He reminded me of carefree young poets I'd met on the reading circuit, and this made me think of Mark, who'd been much more intense at Johnny's age.

Just as I was wondering if I should call Peter, we heard the police sirens. Red flashers blinked at the window as the cruisers and the ambulance went by.

"They'll never get past that dog," Marion said.

"They will shoot him if they have to," Mabel said.

We had been told to wait at Mabel's place for the police, but the cold atmosphere made me jittery. It reminded me of a fisherman's kitchen long ago in Maine. My grandmother and I had called on a woman whose husband was lost at sea. The boat hadn't been found, or he had fallen overboard. I no longer remembered the details, but it seemed to me the man was a distant relation to my grandfather and that was why my grandmother, who generally held herself apart from the fisherfolk, as she called them, had gone calling. That kitchen was just like Mabel's: stark, unadorned, clean. Don't fidget, my grandmother had told me.

"I think I'll wait at the end of the lane for the police," I said.

Marion got up to accompany me, but then sank back in her chair. Mabel put the kettle on.

I didn't have long to wait. A cruiser pulled in a few minutes later, followed by Scottie in his truck. Lady sat beside him. He left her in the truck and hurried over, almost colliding with the OPP officer.

"What's going on here?" He looked at the officer, but addressed me. "Has something happened to my mother?" His bristly hair stuck out and a good whiff of whiskey wafted over in the chilly autumn air.

"Your mother's fine, Scottie. It's your neighbour, Mr. Austin-Wright. We came over to use your phone, that's all."

Scottie looked puzzled. "The old geezer's had a heart attack, has he?" Now he spoke to the officer, who introduced himself as Constable Neil Andersen.

"We don't know what's happened yet, sir. Perhaps if we could go inside you can give me some information." The police radio crackled behind him. I heard the word "dog." But Mabel had told them about Hans.

"Hans was in there with Mr. Austin-Wright," I informed Scottie. "Marion and I found him." I explained as well as I could. Scottie shook his head and looked stunned.

"Let's all go inside," the constable said. "I'll just advise the others over the radio."

"I'll leave Lady in the car, then," Scottie said.

"Where'd you find her?" I asked him. "Your mother was out looking for her when we drove by earlier."

"Oh, she was sitting alongside the road. Likely she took off and decided to wait for me to come along."

Mabel had not only made tea, but she was serving it in china cups, which she must have unearthed from some hidden china cabinet. Or didn't she have enough plain mugs? Marion was still wearing her coat.

"Found Lady," Scottie told his mother. He glanced at the china cups. "She's safe and sound in the truck." He went to the cupboard for a mug, but Mabel set a cup in front of him.

Mabel poured his tea. "Where was she?"

"Up near the highway, sitting on the road, waiting for me. Where are Baby and General?"

"Shut in the front room."

"Best leave them there until the police have finished," Scottie advised.

Constable Andersen's entrance halted the dog talk. He was red-haired with that kind of skin that burns easily. He looked older in the kitchen than he had outside. There were crinkly wrinkles around his eyes. No, he didn't want tea, but he thanked Mabel politely for her offer.

"I understand it was you who called, ma'am," he told her.

"Yes, it was I," she said. "Mrs. Hall and her mother-in-law came and told me they'd gone calling at the nursery and that Mr. Austin-Wright was dead. They said he had been shot and they were frightened of the dog."

"Actually, my name's Archer. I go by Archer— I'm a writer," I explained. "Carolyn Archer. My husband's name is Hall and this is my mother-in-law, Marion Hall." Mabel looked at me. She knew I was a writer, but she probably disapproved of a woman not using her husband's name.

"What time were you at the Austin-Wright residence, ma'am?" Andersen asked me.

"Eight o'clock. It must have been exactly eight, because it was about five to when we met Mabel— Mrs. McGrath— on the road. She was looking for her dog and we spoke to her, which took a few minutes. We wanted to be on time because Mr. Austin-Wright seemed to be a stickler for that kind of thing."

Andersen wrote that down.

"And then we got out of the car and walked to the house. The nursery—there's an office downstairs. We could hear the dog barking and were surprised that Mr. Austin-Wright didn't come to control the dog."

"Did you notice anything? Anyone about?"

"Nothing else," I said. "Just the dog barking. The lights were on upstairs where Mr. Austin-Wright has his apartment. His son's van wasn't there.

"We tried the bell and knocked on the door. The dog was beside himself with fury. But I could see past him and... I saw Mr. Austin-Wright lying on the floor. His eyes were open and there was a hole between his eyes. But it was my mother-in-law who saw the body first."

"That's correct," Marion agreed.

"I gather you knew Mr. Austin-Wright."

"I met him a few years ago, but my daughter-in-law, Carolyn, saw him on the weekend."

"I made an appointment to see him at eight tonight, with my mother-in-law," I said. "We were there to keep the appointment."

"Rather late to be buying plants, wasn't it?"

"We wanted to talk to him about a possible book," I said. "This will sound silly, I know, but a few years ago we met Mr. Austin-Wright at Oktoberfest in Kitchener and learned he had known Anna Anderson in Hanover, the woman who was supposed to be Anastasia."

"I know who you are," the constable said suddenly. "You write cookbooks and you did a whodunit a while back. *Murder in the Kitchen*."

I nodded, not bothering to add that I'd "done" more than one whodunit. "We were going to talk to Mr. Austin-Wright about Anastasia. Or Anna Anderson, whatever you want to call her."

"Anna Anderson was an assumed name," Marion explained. "She used it for the first time in America in the late twenties and it became her legal name. The DNA tests said she wasn't Anastasia, but some people think the tissue was switched."

The young officer was actually writing down "Anastasia" and "Anna Anderson." He looked as if he wanted to continue with this subject, but he turned to Mabel and asked her if she'd noticed anything unusual when she was looking for her dog.

"That's the dog in the truck," Scottie explained. "Lady. She's a nervous old girl— "

"There was nothing unusual," Mabel told Andersen. "The only vehicle I saw was theirs. Mrs. Hall's. I went as far as the nursery driveway, but I heard the dog barking in that crazy way of his and I turned back. Lady would never have been there, with him going on. She's afraid of him."

"But you went to look there?"

"I was worried. If the son, Johnny, had taken the dog with him, Lady might have wandered over. She has a great liking for bone meal."

"For bone meal?"

"They sell bone meal for fertilizer. They have been known to spill it. Lady, however, was not there."

"What time was this, ma'am?"

"About ten minutes before Mrs. Hall and Miss Archer arrived."

"So you went to the lane and heard the dog barking and turned back. Did you think it unusual— to hear the dog barking?"

"The dog's always barking. He is not a nice dog."

Scottie explained about their dogs and told Andersen I had bought a puppy from them.

"Will they shoot the dog?" I asked Andersen, who replied that he didn't know.

"I hope they won't have to shoot Hans," Scottie said. "I wouldn't mind having a go if the police can't handle him. He's not truly vicious, Hans. I could control him, I think."

He started to give a discourse about the treatment of dogs and his philosophy that dogs were better than humans, but Andersen took command and cut him off, asking the McGraths about their neighbours. Mabel told the officer exactly what she had told me, but Scottie was more reticent, saying that people were people and who didn't squabble now and again?

Peter and I often discussed Mabel and Scottie with Mark and Emma in those long winding dog conversations that went all over the place, especially over dinner and wine. The general consensus was that Scottie was a true mama's boy and the big question was: had he ever had a girlfriend? The men said no. The women disagreed. What about the meetings at the union hall? Scottie could have something going with a lusty shop steward. Up to her apartment and bed and then back to mama.

Surprisingly, Andersen felt that perhaps Scottie might be able to help with Hans, saying that, in his opinion, dogs regarded policemen on a par with mailmen. But as he spoke, the ambulance went by. "Let me check on the radio," Andersen said.

"We could all be cooking our alibis now," Scottie said as soon as the police officer had gone to the patrol car to radio. "This is not standard procedure. Is he not supposed to stay with us?"

"You are touched in the head," Mabel told her son. "We're not in a murder book. It is plain what happened."

"What, then?" Scottie wanted to know.

But Mabel wouldn't tell him. I knew she was thinking of Johnny. I was thinking of Johnny, too. Who else could have gotten by the dog?

Andersen returned and said that the dog had been subdued and was being taken to the Humane Society. Scottie said Johnny would at least have his dog now that his father was gone. "That's all right then, but Hans won't like being cooped up. Poor fellow."

"When was the last time you saw the son, John?" Andersen asked Scottie and Mabel. Scottie said he had seen Johnny early in the morning. He had passed Johnny's van on the road. Johnny was apparently going home, Scottie guessed. "He often spends nights with friends of his in Guelph."

"And you, ma'am?"

"His van went by just after Humphrey left for his meeting. That would have been about a quarter after six. We feed the dogs at six, and it was right after that time when he drove up the road. The dogs were having a romp in the field and I saw his van drive by."

"Was he alone?"

"I do not know. I saw the van, that is all. I do not know if he saw me or not."

"I just cannot believe it," Scottie said. "No, I truly cannot! Such a thing is truly unbelievable. I cannot credit it at all, I cannot."

Chapter Five

Scottie wasn't the only incredulous one.

"I do not believe it, I just don't believe it," Peter said when Marion and I finally came home at eleven. "Christ! You two visit this man about Anastasia and he's dead when you arrive."

"Mabel seems to think Austin-Wright's son did his father in," I said, "although Johnny seemed such a nice guy. I hope he didn't do it."

"Nice people kill if they're driven to it," Marion said. "It is strange that he should be killed just as we were to see him about Anastasia."

"I don't believe what I'm hearing," Peter said. Conrad slept peacefully beside him on the couch. He was usually bushed by ten, and it was after eleven.

"It's just odd," Marion said. "That's all. And now I'll never find out what he knew."

"Maybe Johnny can tell us. He told me his father talked about Anastasia a lot."

"Yes, the fellow's father has just died and you want to ask him about Anastasia," Peter said, stroking Conrad. "The story's over," he told Marion. "Finished, kaput. It doesn't matter what he knew if that woman wasn't Anastasia."

"You're getting to be just like Hugh, Peter," Marion said. "Opinionated and bossy."

If there was one thing Peter didn't want, it was to turn into his father, who'd exercised military discipline at home and who considered Peter a wimp.

Peter's opposition to our getting involved with Austin-Wright had been partially because he thought all royalty was so much bunk, but also because he hated trouble and danger. I knew he was thinking we'd get on another royal merry-go-round. Our marriage had undergone strains because of my involvement with Millicent Mulvey, and he didn't want the same thing to happen again.

"Hugh isn't telling me what to do, Peter, and you're not telling me, either," Marion said crisply. "And you might respect my opinion as well."

Peter shut his mouth and got up to open the Dutch cupboard where our television set is stored. Might as well see if the murder made the CKCO news, he said.

George Austin-Wright's death was the lead item. Film footage showed the nursery, and ambulance attendants bringing out a covered body. The reporter did not give Austin-Wright's name, but said he was a long-term resident of the area who lived with his son. "Police officials are not confirming the nature of the killing, but they are investigating. The man's son was absent from the dwelling and police would like to interview him about possible leads."

The phone rang.

"Carolyn and my mother found the body," I heard Peter say. "Yes, that's right. They were supposed to see him at eight and when they got there he had been shot. Don't be nuts, Mark."

At the sound of "Mark," Conrad came to and started yipping.

"This is crazy, Mark," Peter said. "The woman wasn't even Anastasia... I don't believe what I'm hearing. You're a lawyer, for crying out loud, not some uneducated bum. Stop that!" he snapped at Conrad, who was barking now. "You'd better talk to Carolyn. I don't think I can have a rational discussion with you on this thing and Conrad's going crazy because he heard your name."

"Peter thinks I'm crazy," Mark told me when I took the phone, "but someone could have thought this Austin-Wright knew something about the money."

"But she wasn't Anastasia," I reminded him.

"Ah, but if someone believed there was money, even if there wasn't, they might have been afraid he'd divulge what he knew. After we talked, I did a bit of reading up on the subject. This Franziska person had to be briefed by someone intimate with the Romanovs. Whoever was behind her probably told her enough to let the other side know they'd better be careful. Did you know Franziska's brother was referred to as a Communist miner? This was the brother who first said she was his sister, but after she talked to him, he changed his mind. The Communists would have had access to documents, diaries, information about the family. So they find this crazy girl who's a double for Anastasia and get her to go along, or convince her she is Anastasia."

"But why?"

"To keep the Romanovs from the money."

"I thought you said there was no money."

"Well, say there was. As long as this Anna Anderson person was on the scene the money would be tied up, wouldn't it? The Communists wouldn't want the Romanovs to have the big bucks. Money could have gone to restoring the dynasty. They actually discussed restoring the dynasty in Greece with a private army, financed by rich Americans who'd married into the Romanov family. And money aside, the arguments about Anna Anderson divided the Romanovs and caused dissension. She knew enough to make various people believe her and there was enough evidence on her side that taking her case to court was chancy for everyone."

"But she lost all the court cases."

"The decisions were always appealed. The last verdict was *non liquet,* meaning neither proven nor disproven, unsatisfactory to all the parties concerned."

"I thought you were a champion of Franziska, the lumpy farm girl who had them all fooled."

"The farm girl who knew so much. The Polish girl who knew what people in the know had told her. Even if it was Franziska who gave your friend Austin-Wright information about money, that doesn't mean what she told him was incorrect."

"Before you get too carried away with this cabal, Mark, you should know that Mabel sort of hinted she thinks the guy's son did him in. The two didn't get along. Who else could have gotten by that vicious German Shepherd they have?"

"Hmm."

"Hmm all you want. Mabel saw the son's van leaving and she says there wasn't another car until Marion and I came along."

"You'd make a rotten courtroom lawyer. I just find it suspicious that you make a date to talk to him about the Romanovs and he's dead when you get there."

"Did you ever think you should have been a historian instead of a lawyer?"

"You couldn't be a credible historian and seriously discuss this Anastasia business."

"You'll just have to represent Johnny in court if he's charged with his father's murder. You can prove some monarchist agent did it. Your moment of glory."

"If you talk to the kid, give him my number. I can use the business," Mark said.

Before he hung up, Mark said we were all invited for dinner the following night.

I lay awake long after Peter and I went to bed. I had expected to be tense about finding Mr. Austin-Wright's body, but instead I found myself thinking about Franziska Schanzkowska. How could a simple woman from a small village— a woman who had worked in a factory, a plain, ordinary country woman— have been able to fool so many people for so long? For— what— fifty years? No, sixty-four years. She threw herself into the canal in Berlin in 1920 and died in 1984, so that was sixty-four years of being someone else.

I knew little about Pomerania and rural, pre-World War I Germany, but I imagined a tiny village little more than a huddle of houses, a church, an inn, at the crossroads. Farm wagons, all the children sleeping in one bed, the cow brought into part of the house in the winter? Chickens pecking in the yard, sauerkraut and potatoes, pigs, muddy lanes, women with sore red hands, women with aprons.

And in all that, living there: Franziska. She had to be intelligent, ambitious. She liked, as Anastasia did, nature, flowers, animals. Anna Anderson was a vegetarian, I remembered. Maybe she wanted to go to school, but there was no money. She had to work in the fields to contribute to the household. The only future, no matter how intelligent or ambitious she was, would have meant marriage, a family, and more toil in the fields. A peasant husband, someone rough and ready who demanded supper on the table promptly at six before falling asleep at eight...

Escape to Berlin then, to work in a factory. She wasn't beautiful, but she had good manners. Maybe in her family, in the village, they teased her about putting on airs, about thinking she was better than other people... The war broke out, Russia and Germany were enemies. She had always been fascinated with the Kaiser and his family. Her own family would have had a picture of the Kaiser, I imagined. She could have seen the Kaiser in parades, would have read about the Kaiser in the newspapers, known about their children, and as she worked on the grenade factory line in Berlin the fact that she was contributing to the war effort, helping the Kaiser, might have added to her secret knowledge that she was meant for something better.

Perhaps, even, there was a family legend that the Schanzkowskis came from better things, that they had fallen on hard times. Maybe she imagined that a grandparent was the illegitimate offspring of a prince.

And then the injuries to her head and arm in the factory. Life was over, there would be no respite. She wanted only to end it— where was the hope? What was the good of knowing she was capable of so much more if she could not achieve anything?

Depressed, she needed psychiatric help. She was found legally insane, with delusions of grandeur. When, a few years later, she threw herself into the canal and was rescued, she knew if she gave her name, she would be committed to an asylum for life.

Better an asylum for a little while. No one knew who she was. She was called Miss Unknown, a woman with a mysterious past. She could be anything or anyone she liked. And there, in the asylum, was a magazine with photos of the Tsar's family. Someone pointed out that Miss Unknown looked so much like Anastasia, who, rumour had it, escaped the slaughter.

And maybe— why couldn't she be Anastasia? Her past life was a bad dream: she could play the part, could practise being Anastasia, could imagine Anastasia's tragedy as hers. And really, there was so much similarity, so much could-have-been. The sea around Danzig could have been near Finland, where the Russian imperial family sailed in their yacht. She knew, too, what it was to have an ill, religious mother. She could imagine the lilacs in Alexandra's private room, the footmen and the soldiers in uniform who looked so much like the Kaiser's soldiers. She always liked men in uniforms, strong, tall men, not brawny rough farmers, but straight and disciplined men in immaculate tunics and boots.

Poor Anastasia! Anna felt a deep sympathy thinking of Anastasia in the snows of Siberia, and understood how it all had been: the regular lessons, the orderly days, the embroidery and language lessons (Franziska had taught herself a little English), the tea in the evening, the lamplight falling on the cots where the girls slept. Oh, it was boring for Anastasia, but sweet, too, and comforting to be in her place.

Evenings, when she closed her eyes in the asylum ward, she pictured Anastasia's mother, Alexandra, who had been a German princess from Hesse. And there was Nicholas, who loved his wife so much. And little Alexis, the hemophiliac Heir to the Throne, in his sailor suit. You belong to us, Nicholas and Alexandra told her, and she knew that if she were to meet Alexandra on the street, the Empress would know her. But of course the Empress was dead. They were all dead. Except Anastasia, who survived the massacre and was spirited out of Russia.

A soldier carried her away, a soldier who loved her. A soldier who maybe rescued her before the others were slaughtered. But this part, like images of Pomerania, was hazy. She could not think of it, could not imagine dear Tatiana, Marie, Olga, and Alexis shot and stabbed with bayonets.

She only knew she could be Anastasia.

A new patient at the asylum confirmed the likeness. The woman, Clara, had lived in Russia, had seen the Grand Duchesses. Tatiana, the woman called her, and Miss Unknown did not correct her: the Anastasia identity was too nebulous, too shadowy. She knew she had to guard it well, but while Clara talked about Russia and all she knew about the imperial family, Miss Unknown felt how it must have been, Anastasia showing herself with her family to the cheering crowds: the girls in their light dresses, hats. Rasputin and Alexandra's friend Anna Vioubova, who had a house on the palace grounds at Tsarskoe Selo. All Russia gossiped about Rasputin and the Empress, Clara said, and Miss Unknown was indignant that anyone should criticize her beloved Alexandra...

Released, Clara contacted the monarchists, who soon arrived at the asylum. Afraid, Miss Unknown would not show her face in case they said she was not Anastasia. Would not an impostor be only too eager to impress them? the monarchists asked themselves. This shy girl was so like Anastasia, but entirely inappropriate as an impostor. There had been other impostors, all quickly uncovered. This girl had no front teeth. They must have been knocked out by rifle blows, not extracted because of decay and pain, as her enemies said, or to change her looks.

She would not speak Russian, it was too painful for her after what the Russians did to her family. But she understood Russian, the words sounding Polish although the Schanzkowskis prided themselves on being German.

Not the Schanzkowskis— no; that was so far away. She could make those old memories go away by concentrating hard on Alexandra... and the Dowager Empress, Grandma, babushka in Russian, who looked so tiny in the newspaper pictures, but who once sat on Alexis' bed (the newspapers said) and helped him to peel an apple like any other grandmother. That was on the imperial yacht, *The Standart*, where the girls roller-skated with the young officers.

Clara said they had expected some of the Tsar's daughters to marry into the British royal family.

"Then war came," Miss Unknown said, "but such marriages were discussed. I know they were talked about. Papa and the King of England were cousins, you know. No one could tell them apart when they were together, and their mothers were sisters."

That was what she called Nicholas: Papa.

"She knows so much," Clara told the monarchists. Berlin was filled with monarchists and White Russians. "She knows the most intimate details about life at court."

Russian monarchists, Baron von Kleist and his wife, took Miss Unknown to live with them. There are rumours, they told her, that the Grand Duchess Anastasia escaped to Romania. Was this true? But she would not talk of that. It was too painful; it was far better to concentrate on Anastasia and mama and Alexis in the room filled with lilacs. Recalling Romania, a primitive country, was too much like thinking about that other place with the snow in the winter and the big room with its tiled coal stove that always smelled of wet wool and sweat.

"I cannot talk about it, I cannot," Miss Unknown said.

"There was a soldier," the monarchists persisted. "Didn't a soldier rescue the Grand Duchess? She had jewels sewn into her clothes and they lived on those."

It was easier to think of the soldier. A peasant, but noble underneath, handsome, virile, but perhaps simple? A soldier loyal to the Tsar would risk his own life to rescue a daughter of the Tsar and protect her. Yes, but living forever with a simple peasant... no, she did not like this. The soldier would have died, protecting her...

Protecting Anastasia.

Yes, she was Anastasia. She admitted it to the von Kleists.

She fell ill with TB, her arm was infected, she was hospitalized. The Tsar's sister, the Grand Duchess Olga, came from Copenhagen to visit her in the clinic. Gilliard, the imperial children's tutor, visited with his wife, Shura, who had been the girls' nurse. They were not sure if the invalid was Anastasia. Yes? No? The invalid had a bunion like Anastasia had.

After a few months, Olga said the invalid was not Anastasia. But not a definite impostor. Others believed: Olga had sent letters to Miss Unknown, presents. Newspaper articles were written while "Anastasia" recuperated in a sanatorium in the mountains. Tatiana Botkin, daughter of Dr. Botkin, the physician killed with the imperial family in Siberia, visited and said the patient was Anastasia. But when the newspapers printed a picture, a Berlin woman came forward and identified Anastasia as *Franziska Schanzkowska*.

Detectives visited Franziska's family in her own village in Pomerania. Felix, Franziska's brother, came to the castle where "Anastasia" had recently moved and identified his sister.

But how could that be? Anastasia was remote at first, but then the past returned. It was terrible— the slaughter and the flight from Russia and the small village in Pomerania were all mixed up in her mind. "Do not speak about these things," she told Felix. "I do not want to hear about it. That is all in the past and has nothing whatsoever to do with the present!"

Felix said the woman was not his sister. Why should he hurt Franziska's chances?

And after that, famous and notorious, how could she stop being Anastasia? I wondered. Exposed as Franziska, she would have been jailed for fraud or committed for life to an insane asylum. A crazy woman. With her known face, she could not become anyone else.

And why should she be anyone else? She was Anastasia. More and more memories were coming back. People knew she was Anastasia. Who else could she be? *You are Anastasia*, they said.

But later, when she grew old and senile, did Franziska ever return? I wondered. She had married an American history professor who was twenty years younger— more like twenty-five years younger than *Franziska*— and he would not hire nurses to look after her, saying his wife didn't want strangers around. She had become ornery and difficult. Her husband believed her to the end, but did she sometimes yell at him that she was really Franziska?

"I am Franziska, a Polish peasant, a demented factory worker!"

"No, you are Anastasia! The daughter of His Imperial Highness Tsar Nicholas II of Russia!"

She died in a hospital. I wondered if a nurse or doctor who had read the books about Anastasia ever whispered "Franziska"...

It would have been a cruel thing to do.

But a relief, too: she could die under the name she had been born with, which was all "Anastasia" said she had ever desired.

Chapter Six

Emma was a superb cook; she had acquired this skill during the commune days. While the guys were stoned and drumming, strumming and singing in the barn, she coped with the mounds of cabbages, turnips, apples and sacks of flour. It goes without saying that only a woodstove was deemed suitable for the cook-in-residence.

Emma's repertoire had broadened considerably, but she had a woodstove again, albeit a modern model from the Elmira Stove Works. But that was the only thing similar to the old days. Mark and Emma's hobby farm with its renovated farmhouse was a long way from the draughty, dirty shell the commune-ites had inhabited.

I loved her house with its large, sunny kitchen and eclectic mixture of early Canadiana, antiques, and just plain colourful, comfortable furniture. The summer kitchen had become a studio for Emma's quilt making and the pantry was Mark's study. The place always smelled of homemade bread, soup, or the wine Emma and Mark concocted from the berry patch. Books and plants were everywhere.

Dinner was always a kitchen affair. Guests sipped wine and maybe made a salad while Emma chopped and minced and Mark and Thomas set the long pine table with red dishes. There was even a ginger cat, Pumpkin, curled in a chair. Kelly dozing on a braided mat by the stove made the tableau complete.

As always, Kelly was overjoyed to see her brother. With one leap, Conrad was out of the car, and as usual, he jumped on her back. Both of them grinned like idiots until Thomas pulled them apart and threw a ball for them to chase.

"Forget any civilized greeting," Mark said, shaking Marion's hand in the yard. "You can see what happens when Peter and Carolyn bring the monster over."

"Our monster and your nymphomaniac," Peter said. "How's the cold?" he asked Thomas.

"Okay. We're getting Kelly fixed so she can't have puppies," Thomas piped up. "Dad says if Kelly and Conrad breed they'll have retarded puppies," he told Marion. "What's a nymphomaniac?" he asked Peter, whose reply was cut off by Marion.

"Look, they're not bringing the ball back."

"That's because Kelly won't drop it and she can run faster than Conrad," Thomas said. "She can run faster than me. We have races all the time. She understands 'On your mark, get set, go.' She sits until I say 'Go.' But she won't do it for Dad because he hits her with a newspaper when she doesn't listen."

"Enough dog talk," Mark said, turning red. "Let's go in and sample the vino."

"Want me to show you?" Thomas asked Marion.

"Maybe Mrs. Hall would rather have a glass of wine, Thomas," Mark suggested. "And you'd better come in and wash up soon."

"But I'd like to see the race," Marion said. "Really, I would, Mark."

Peter said: "I've got to see this, too. Maybe we can teach Conrad to do the same thing."

"I, however, will have a glass of wine," I said. "Try to keep Conrad from chomping on any wood!"

Emma, wearing a blue apron smudged with flour, was de-veining shrimp and sipping a glass of white wine. Something garlicky was bubbling on the stove, and mingled with this was the smell of cloves and pumpkin.

"Help yourself to the wine. I'd pour you a glass but my hands are distinctly fishy."

"Fried shrimp?"

"No, spicy oriental soup with shredded spinach. That's for starters. I made the stock this morning. And then lamb. Good old Canadian pumpkin pie for dessert. Around the world with Emma."

"Can I do anything?" I poured myself a glass of wine.

"If you're really ambitious you can tear the spinach. Where's everyone else?"

"Thomas wants to show them how Kelly can race."

"Those two," Emma said, looking past my shoulder to the window. Peter was trying to get Conrad to sit, but Conrad kept barking and jumping around, apparently not understanding his commands. Thomas was in on the act, instructing Conrad as well, while Marion, looking cold, held Kelly's ball. Emma sighed.

"Anything wrong?"

"No." She finished the last shrimp and threw the de-veiner into the sink. "Well, actually yes, but don't say anything. I haven't even told Mark yet."

"What?"

"I had a phone call from Thomas' father this afternoon. His real father, that is, or should I say birth father? I haven't heard from him for years and this afternoon while I was busily, happily, innocently putting the damn pumpkin pies in the oven the phone rings and it's him."

She'd barely discussed her ex-husband with me, beyond saying that it was a short marriage and that both of them knew on their honeymoon in Venice that it wouldn't work.

"He only found me because we put our phone number in my name so Mark wouldn't be bothered at home. Thomas' father called directory assistance and got our number."

"But Mark's adopted Thomas. Your ex must have signed papers or something and have known where you were."

Emma gathered the shrimp shells and wiped the butcher block counter that separated the eating area from the kitchen.

"Franz isn't Thomas' father," Emma said. "I was still legally married to him when Thomas was born, but Thomas' father is a guy from Minnesota I met on a cruise in Finland. I spent a week with him and became pregnant. I could have had an abortion easily enough in Holland, but I was thirty-three and I'd already had one abortion. I was pregnant when I left Mark that summer."

"I didn't know that."

"Nope. No one did. Not even Mark, although I told him when we got back together."

"Mark is fine with Thomas."

"Mostly. He can be short." She poured herself more wine. I didn't say anything and she didn't add to this revelation.

"So what's the problem with this guy from Minnesota?"

"Jensen. He wants to see Thomas."

"But if the adoption went through— "

"I listed Franz as Thomas' father. Franz signed the papers, as a favour. I had no idea where Jensen was, as a matter of fact, and as Mark pointed out, Franz was Thomas' legal father."

"So Mark knows."

"Mark knew all along. You're the only other person I've told. But Mark didn't tell his partner at the firm who drew up the papers the truth."

"Jensen knew you were pregnant?"

"He came back to Amsterdam six months later, on his way home from India. The deal was that I wouldn't press for child support, and he wouldn't interfere in our lives in any way. He was scared I'd sue him for support. I'll wait to add the shrimp and spinach. They'll all want drinks before we sit down."

"What did you tell Jensen?"

"To go to hell. Now he says he has rights!"

"I wonder why he's changed his tune?"

"I wouldn't know. Maybe I should have talked to him instead of hanging up. I'm afraid to answer the phone now, in case it's him. And what if Thomas answers and this strange man says, 'Hi son, this is your dad!'? Mark and I agree that we'll have to tell him the truth some day, but..."

Emma was interrupted by the banging of the door, followed by Thomas racing into the house with the dogs at his heels.

"Conrad can't do it!" he yelled, opening the fridge and taking out two dog treats which he threw to the dogs.

"I think you should tell Mark about the call," I whispered, as the others trooped in.

Mark's loquaciousness, fuelled by wine and food, was a good shield for Emma's ill-ease. The subject, naturally, was Anastasia. Mark and Marion did most of the talking, speculating how a simple Polish woman could have pulled off what Marion, drinking more wine than was usual for her, called the "mystery of the century." Mark reiterated his premise that even if Anna Anderson wasn't Anastasia, she still had important information, which George Austin-Wright might have known.

And the reason for this, Mark speculated, could have been that whoever gave her the information knew that the real Anastasia was alive, and that the information was just enough to make Anna Anderson's enemies fear her enough to take her seriously, thus making the real Anastasia's life safe from the Bolsheviks.

Marion found this theory fascinating ("This is just so interesting!"), and added that there had been real evidence, attested to with affidavits, that the real Anastasia had fled to Romania. An officer had assisted a wagon said to contain the wounded Grand Duchess to cross a border and later received money for his help. So— if the real

Anastasia had escaped to Romania, Anna Anderson's mention of Romania would have meant a lot to both her enemies and supporters.

"So you are saying that whoever gave Anna Anderson the information knew about the real Anastasia's survival?" Marion asked. "Forgetting for a moment that I still think Anna Anderson was Anastasia."

"Right. It's a possibility. And the people who were against her had to consider that she was perhaps, just perhaps, Anastasia, and thus they had no interest in finding the real Anastasia."

"Unless Anna Anderson's enemies knew where the real Anastasia was and that was why they knew she was not Anastasia," Marion parried. "And there's the mystery of Mr. Austin-Wright looking a great deal like Tsar Nicholas, not to mention the mystery of his death."

"Yet there's no evidence his death had anything to do with what he knew about the Romanovs," I said.

"But," Mark said, "you have to admit there's a possibility. You're going to see him about a book at the same time as the second DNA test results were announced. You have to admit, there could be something in it."

"Johnny said his father'd lost his license. Maybe they fought about Johnny taking off in the van when his father wanted to go somewhere. One thing could have led to another."

"But why would Austin-Wright want to go anywhere?" Mark asked. "He was waiting for you."

"That's right," Marion agreed. "He was waiting for us to tell us what he knew about Anastasia. Maybe Anna Anderson knew where the real Anastasia was. What do you think?"

"Circles and circles," Peter said, turning to Thomas to discuss dogs.

I gradually joined the Anastasia discussion and no one except me noticéd that Emma didn't say a word. When she began clearing the table, Mark— still talking— automatically rose to help but she impatiently waved him back to his chair. Nor did she want my assistance with the coffee and dessert.

"Let's take the dogs for a run," Peter suggested to Thomas. Mark paused in his dissertation on the Russian monarchists to object that it was a school night and Thomas had better get to bed.

"Just this once won't hurt," Emma said quietly, pouring coffee. Thomas grabbed his jacket and was out of the door before Mark could object. He wouldn't cause a scene with guests present. But seeing the displeasure on his face and Emma's anxious eyes, I worried that this happily-ever-romance wasn't so happy after all.

Mark phoned at ten the next morning to tell me that Johnny Austin-Wright had been arrested the previous night for impaired driving on the way back from London.

"Impaired driving! The little idiot, with all his other troubles."

"Ah, but he didn't know. He didn't know a thing."

"I suppose you're going to represent him. And how did you find out so soon?"

"Connections, to answer your second question. I know the cops. They were looking for him, and when they caught him his name came up on the screen, so to speak. As for the other question, I called London and I'm driving down there as soon as I hang up. Ordinarily they'd let him go after a twelve-hour suspension, but they're holding him until the OPP guys arrive."

"So they do suspect him?"

"What do you think?"

"Did you talk to him?"

"Did do. Poor kid. He didn't know the OPP were on their way. He had just woken up. He's not going to say anything until I get there. He'd just been informed of his father's death before I called."

"What was he doing in London? And impaired driving! He must have known how strict the cops are these days."

"He told me he was visiting friends. He didn't say much else."

"Maybe he was heading for the border. Detroit's not that far from London."

"He was on his way back."

"Don't tell me you're actually considering the Romanov angle in all this? People will think you're nuts. It could be just a simple murder," I said, although I hated the thought that Johnny could have done it.

"I like how you put that."

"You know what I mean."

"Well, first things first. I'd better go and meet my client."

"It was murder, wasn't it? Not suicide."

"They didn't find the weapon. But listen, before I hang up, give Emma a call and tell her I'll be late, will you? She wasn't home and she must have forgotten to switch the answering machine on. You can explain to her better than my secretary can."

I phoned repeatedly, but Emma didn't answer and the answering machine remained turned off. But of course she was probably there, jumping each time the telephone rang and not answering in case it was Jensen. Nor would she want him leaving messages on the machine, in case Thomas or Mark played the tape back. I would have to drive out to see her, I thought, and luckily Marion was heading for the library, so I could talk to Emma alone.

She'd have to tell Mark about Jensen's re-emergence in her life, I thought, as I drove to Eden Mills. It was beginning to rain and for once Conrad settled quietly in the back seat. When I turned into the town itself he roused himself, recognizing the scenery, realizing that he was on his way to see the love of his life.

"Back, back. No, no. Conrad, sit!" I was tempted to whack him, but I screamed instead, loudly, which stunned him. Momentarily.

I hit him on the rump with my purse, harder than I realized, and with a shocked whelp, he huddled into the seat.

"Oh, Conrad. I'm sorry, I'm sorry." I thought of Thomas saying that Mark hit Kelly with a newspaper and suddenly I felt a sense of foreboding, as if I would find something terrible at Emma's house.

The place looked sad and grey in the rain. Her car was there. Feeling guilty for hitting him, I didn't restrain Conrad when he began barking again, my assault apparently forgotten. At least Emma would know from Kelly's barking that we were there, and not Jensen.

She answered the door looking puffy-faced, as if she'd just woken up. She wore an old track suit and her hair wasn't combed. Emma always used a little mascara because her lashes were so light, but she hadn't bothered to do so today.

She made coffee while I relayed Mark's message. She had honestly forgotten to turn the machine on again, she said. She didn't seem interested in Johnny Austin-Wright— and I wouldn't have been either, in her shoes.

Conrad and Kelly raced off, chasing each other through the downstairs rooms. The roast pan from last night was still soaking in the sink.

Emma excused herself while the coffee dripped and returned with her hair combed and her mascara in place. I thought of her mascara years ago. It had come in a little red plastic box, and you had to moisten the applicator. I remembered her telling me that even at the commune Mark had never seen her without her mascara.

"I need some coffee to wake up anyway," she said. "I slept in this morning and Mark just nuked what was left from last night and got Thomas off to school. Too much red wine. I should have stuck to the white."

She spread a white embroidered cloth on the butcher block counter for the coffee cups. She always did this, even for a casual drop-in cup of coffee. I knew she had embroidered this particular piece of linen as a girl as a Christmas gift for her grandmother and that she'd had it returned when the grandmother died.

"What're you going to do about Jensen?" I asked.

"I'm going to get an unlisted telephone. We've been talking about that anyway. Some of Mark's less respectable clients have our number. Mark gave it to them in case they landed in jail or something. I'll just tell Mark I finally got around to arranging it."

"I bet you're sorry you told me about Jensen. But you know I won't say anything. To anyone. But I wish you'd tell Mark. He'd have some ideas."

"Jensen says the adoption was illegal."

"That's what I mean. Mark would know about that."

"Sometimes I think Mark wouldn't be so unhappy over the adoption being annulled."

"That's crazy."

"I think he's much too strict with Thomas sometimes. He says I babied him. But it was just the two of us, and in Holland my old Aunt Heidi looked after him. Mark hated his father for his strict ways and I never dreamed Mark would be just like him. It was great when we were first together, when Thomas was younger, but now it's 'Homework before play, Thomas,' and 'Don't you think you can do better than 78% on the math test?'"

"That doesn't sound so dreadful. It's just— fatherly."

"The trouble is, Thomas isn't a scholar. A good average kid, but no Einstein. I'd rather see him happy, enjoying his childhood, than worried about his schoolwork. You've heard those stories about kids in Hong Kong and Japan throwing themselves out of windows because they didn't do well on a test."

"Come on, Emma. It's never going to be like that."

"But you know what the real thing is?" she went on as if she hadn't heard me. "I think Mark doesn't really feel that Thomas is his son. If Thomas went somewhere else, Mark wouldn't try to find him, as Jensen— awful as he is— is doing. I know that. I think it was a big let-down to Mark when Thomas started Grade One and had trouble learning to read. That started it."

"Maybe you and Mark should go for counselling."

"Mark wouldn't. Don't kid yourself. He likes to be the big liberal thinker, the modern humanist, but when it comes down to it, he's turning into his father. I bet he'll even go into politics and it won't be on the NDP ticket. That's why he ran for the School Board, you know. I bet if I turned into his mother, joining this and that, playing golf, Mark wouldn't mind a bit. And his mother's a problem, too. She hasn't taken to Thomas, not like she would her own. We tried, you know, to have a baby. Went to a specialist and so on and so forth, but nothing. And of course I had that abortion long ago. Maybe I shouldn't have told Mark about that. He didn't know at the time..."

"I think you're making more of everything because of Jensen contacting you. Mark would probably be the same with his natural son. Who's had a totally happy childhood? There's always something. My grandmother brought me up and it wasn't too bad, but I would have run away if I'd had to live with my mother. When I visited her in Chicago when I was thirteen she had a young boyfriend and made me say I was her sister, for instance. And think about your own childhood."

"Most of it spent on my knees, as I remember. And that's another problem, a big one. If my parents find out about Jensen..." She shook her head. Emma's parents now thought Mark, being a lawyer, was wonderful. "They might even tell Mark's mother the truth, out of revenge."

"You'd see things differently if you told Mark. The threat of Jensen arriving on the scene might reinforce Mark's sense of father-hood. Or ownership, if you want to call it that. You know. 'He's not going to get his hands on my son.'"

"Maybe you're right," Emma sighed.

"Anyway, all marriages have rough spots. Peter and I came close to breaking up, after I got involved in that Millicent story. He really hated me having secrets from him. I think that nagged at him, knowing I kept things from him. That's another reason to tell Mark. Secrets do nothing but fester."

"I told Mark about the abortion and I know it's been on his mind ever since, especially now that I can't get pregnant. The biological clock's ticking away."

"Just tell Mark. Think about it, anyway. Let Mark share the worry at least."

"Perhaps I will," Emma sighed.

But I doubted that she would tell Mark about Jensen.

A police cruiser was parked in front of our place when I got home. I left Conrad in the car. Any uniform spells "letter carrier" to him and I didn't want him attacking a cop.

Neil Andersen was having tea with Marion in the kitchen. A pile of my books, which Marion must have dragged out, sat beside the teapot on the pine table.

"I'm impressed," he said, shaking hands. "I had no idea you had so many books out. I guess I didn't pay enough attention to what they said about you on the back of *Murder in the Kitchen*."

"One seems to have led to the other," I said. "Cookbooks and murder mysteries. One day I'll write a real book. Actually, it was Marion who got me into mysteries. She kept saying I should try one and I did."

"You would have written one anyway, sooner or later," Marion said, pouring me a cup of tea. "It seemed a shame not to put all that knowledge about early Canadian food and customs to another use."

My mysteries were set in the early nineteen-hundreds, and Andersen asked if I was writing anything new, and where did I get my ideas? The usual questions. Anastasia came up, with Marion doing most of the talking. Andersen said if I ever needed any help about police procedures to call on him. Marion told him about Hugh.

We could have gone on like this forever, but at last Andersen, with reluctance it seemed to me, turned to the subject of the murder. He seemed so likeable and good-natured, sitting there with his hands wrapped around his mug, that I was tempted to tell him about Mark's phone call. Andersen had that kind of friendly, easy manner and open face that invited confidences, but I decided to say nothing.

He went over the same territory he had covered on the night of the murder. No, we hadn't noticed anyone around. There were no other vehicles, no customers.

Had we told anyone about our appointment with Mr. Austin-Wright in advance?

Only Peter, I replied, and we'd mentioned it to our friends, Mark and Emma. It turned out that Neil knew Mark; that is to say, he knew him professionally, from going to court.

"And I imagine the son, Johnny, would have known," Marion said.

"Or perhaps not," I mused. "I think Mr. Austin-Wright would not have been entirely forthcoming with Johnny. But that's just a guess. Sorry. I'm speaking off the top of my head."

"You met Johnny on the weekend," Neil prompted.

"Yes, when I dropped in to see Mr. Austin-Wright about the Anastasia thing. Johnny seemed a nice young man. Relaxed, easy to get along with. He said his father had wanted him to write about Anastasia, too."

"And did he?"

"No, he thought it was nonsense. I got the impression that his father spent a lot of time talking about Anastasia the way some people go on about the war or the Kennedy conspiracy. Johnny had heard it all a million times before, it seemed."

"Then you spoke to Mr. Austin-Wright."

"Yes. Johnny took me upstairs. Mr. Austin-Wright wasn't too pleased to see me at first. He seemed annoyed with Johnny for interrupting his opera. He was listening to Wagner through headphones. I don't think he remembered me, but when I mentioned Anastasia, he said he recalled meeting me. I don't know if he did or not. I kind of think he didn't, but he was just as keen on the Anastasia story as when we originally met. I don't know if you want to hear all this."

"Go on," Neil said.

"He said he'd be killed if he told the truth about the Romanovs and their money. The Tsar was supposed to have a fortune hidden away, in England I think, although no one knows very much about the money. Some people said it didn't exist after the first world war because the Tsar brought all the money back to Russia. Mr. Austin-Wright felt that this money was the source of Anastasia's misery and lack of recognition. Anna Anderson's misery, I should say, or Franziska Schanzkowska's misery, because that's who she turned out to be. It's hard to believe this old story could have anything to do with Mr. Austin-Wright's death. Why shouldn't he tell his story? A lot of books have been written about the subject. I think he was only trying to make himself seem important."

"Did you see Johnny again?"

"He came upstairs when his father and I were talking and asked for change. I think the father controlled the money. Mr. Austin-Wright seemed annoyed at the intrusion, or maybe he just wanted me to see that he was in charge."

"Not a pleasant man," Neil ventured.

"An eccentric one," I said. "But that's all I can tell you, except that Johnny did mention that his father had lost his driver's license for being impaired. His father could have been cross that Johnny was

73

going away, leaving him stranded at the nursery, but on the other hand, he was waiting to see us, so he wouldn't have wanted to go anywhere that night."

"And you originally met him some time ago?"

"A few years ago at the Concordia Club in Kitchener at Oktoberfest. Marion was there, too, as well as a cousin from England. And Peter. We all had a lot of beer, except for Peter, who was driving."

I let Marion continue. She told the story well: Austin-Wright's passion on the subject of Anna Anderson, his tears when I expressed the opinion that he looked like the Tsar, and the fact that he kissed my hand when he left.

"Would you really have written a book with him?" Neil asked me.

"I doubt it. Marion?"

She shrugged and said she wasn't the writer, I was.

"I thought he lived in his own world pretty much," I said. "He wanted to write about Anna Anderson but he hadn't read any of the books written about her."

"Anderson, hmm."

"It was a name picked out of a hat to evade the press in the late nineteen-twenties. It became her legal name until she married a history professor in the States in the late sixties. Her husband always believed her claim."

"He became as eccentric as she was," Marion added. "She turned his house, a fine house in a good neighbourhood, into chaos. She had about forty cats and they never cleaned up after the pets or cut the grass. Their neighbours were always taking them to court."

"Isn't this nuts?" I asked Neil. "You're here asking us questions about going to Mr. Austin-Wright's home and here we are talking about Anna Anderson."

"It does explain your involvement with Mr. Austin-Wright, and it tells something about his background."

"He had an English name, but his mother was German. They lived near Anna Anderson in Hanover, in Germany. That's why he called his business the Old Hanover Nursery. Was it open for business that night? Mabel said she didn't hear or see any other cars, but she could have missed hearing them when she was feeding the dogs."

"The place was only open Friday night. They were closed the other nights," Neil said.

"Well, whoever killed him couldn't have known we were coming," I said. "It was taking an awful chance if the killer knew, in case we came early or something."

"Or they knew and wanted us to find the body," Marion said.

"But there's the problem of the dog," I said. "Someone had to get by the dog. Johnny seems the obvious culprit, but I just can't see him killing his father."

Neil closed his notebook. He looked thoughtful. "You can never tell what people will do. You see the most ordinary people, husbands mowing the lawn and wives taking the kids to the park. You know, middle-class, ordinary people living ordinary lives in ordinary houses. Then, bang, there's a murder-suicide or the guy's holed up inside with a rifle and the neighbours are saying, 'I never noticed anything. They were friendly and quiet, good neighbours.' Turns out the wife has a lover and the husband goes bananas. The druggies and dope pushers are predictable. Sooner or later someone gets knifed or robs a drugstore, but people in general— you never know what is really going on or what can happen."

"You sound soured on humanity," I said. I thought of Emma and Mark and had a sudden image of police cruisers arriving at three a.m., Emma in her nightgown weeping in the doorway.

"Being a policeman does something to a person," Marion said.

"Even in little Meredith. We don't have big-time drug pushers, but there are the domestic fights and the drunken squabbles. I'm glad Hugh's retired. I think the police need sabbaticals every so many years, just so they don't become too jaded."

"Not a bad idea," Andersen said. "I could use one every other year, I think."

"How long have you been with the OPP?" Marion wanted to know.

"Eighteen years this November. Three years around Guelph. My father was a minister in Saskatchewan. Preacher's kid. My mother taught piano. My parents were English. The last thing they wanted me to do was to become a cop, so that's what I did."

"And if your father had been a police officer, you would have become a bookstore owner like my son, Peter," Marion said.

"Or I could have become a criminal," Neil said. "The police chief's son at home was convicted last year of selling stolen cars. He was trouble even as a kid. They had the jail attached to the chief's house and the chief locked his son in one time, but his mother released him.

"The poor woman had to cook the prisoners' meals," Neil added, with a grin.

"That's one blessing I've been spared," Marion said.

"It was extra income. Sadie, that was her name."

"Why did the chief lock his son up?"

"He stole a dog and tried to sell it to Americans at a local campground. Someone almost bought him, too, but they were suspicious because the dog had just been groomed. A poodle, the thief said, purebred, sent by train from a breeder in Quebec. The owner was this retired school teacher who drove Pierre into Saskatoon once a month to have his hair clipped or shaved or whatever they do to poodles. Scot, the chief's son, didn't have a brain in his head. Like most criminals." He glanced at his watch. "I'd better be on my way. I've taken enough of your time."

"You tell good stories," I said, following him to the door.

He paused in the living room. "Nice place. Lots of books. I've always wanted to live in a house like this but I never seem to be anywhere long enough to fix anything up. Did you add the kitchen, the cathedral ceiling and all?"

"We had the back addition put on. We were really cramped before we added that, just the kitchen, front room and two bedrooms and a tiny cubby-hole where I kept my desk. They call these old stone houses Ontario cottages. Worker's places, but they're in now. The workers live in suburbia."

"Like me," Neil sighed. "Well, if I don't meet you again, good luck with the writing."

Conrad went nuts when he saw Neil in his uniform. I waited until the cruiser was out of sight before I released the beast, but even then he bellowed his protests in the direction the cruiser had gone.

I had a feeling I'd see Neil again.

Chapter Seven

Johnny Austin-Wright was arrested for the murder of his father that afternoon. His van had been impounded on the impaired driving charge and the London police had found a weapon under the front seat. For "weapon," translate a Luger service revolver from World War II, according to Mark. The revolver had recently been fired and ballistic tests proved that the gun had been used to kill Mr. Austin-Wright.

"So it seems like an open-and-shut case," I said. I was disappointed and saddened. I had only met Johnny the one time, but I really hadn't thought he was guilty.

"And he says he didn't do it," Mark told us. "He swears he has no idea how the gun came to be there. Never saw the gun before in his life, he claims. He says someone planted it."

"That's kind of far-fetched," Peter said. "But what else can the guy say? It's obvious he did it. He had the opportunity and probably the motive, too. Living with his father couldn't have been a bed of roses. So they get in a fight, the son shoots his father and takes off. And don't forget the dog."

"The crown would probably reduce the charge to manslaughter," Mark said, "but I don't know. Johnny says he didn't do it. But to prove he didn't do it is something else."

"The dog cinches it for me," Peter said.

Mark shook his head and sipped his Scotch. He'd come to our place straight from London. Rumpled and hungry, he gladly accepted my offer of nuked lasagna. I wondered if he'd called Emma, and I wondered if the possibility that Johnny had killed his father made him think about his own relationship with Thomas.

"From what I've heard about the dog no one else could have gotten past him. I bet if someone tried to hurt me, even little Conrad would go straight for the jugular," Peter said with pride, patting Conrad, who dozed by his feet.

"What do you mean, even Conrad?" I asked. "Especially Conrad would be more like it."

Mark didn't join the dog banter.

"Johnny's pretty worried about that dog," Mark said. "Hans is at the Humane Society now, but how long will they keep him before having him, as they put it, 'adopted'? Does that sound like a murderer to you?"

"Hitler loved his dog, too," Peter said.

Mark ignored this. "If I can get bail for him there won't be a problem, of course. I told him I'd rescue Hans and take him home if he didn't get bail."

"What? Are you nuts? That dog's vicious," I said. "And what about Emma?"

"We've got lots of room," Mark shrugged. "If I have to, I'll rig up some kind of kennel. What was I supposed to do? Johnny's been charged with murder and he's got other worries. He shouldn't have to worry about his dog."

"Remind me to call on you if I ever get arrested for anything," I said. I was aghast for Emma. "You not only provide legal services but kennel services as well. I don't know how you can do this to Emma."

"She won't mind. And the dog'll be company for Kelly."

His sister's name roused Conrad, who ran barking joyously to the front door.

"You're nuts," I told Mark. "Next you'll be saying that you think the gun was planted because of some big conspiracy about Anastasia and the Romanov money."

The look on Mark's face told me this was exactly what he was considering.

"I give up," I said, and went to the kitchen to make myself a cup of tea. I was shaking with anger. I shouldn't have done it, but I called Emma to tell her that Mark was here and to inform her what he was planning to do.

As soon as I finished dialling, I realized she probably wouldn't answer anyway, because it might be Jensen. But she picked up the phone on the first ring.

Mark had called her from a pay phone on the highway, she informed me, and as for the dog—

"What does it matter? I don't care." She sounded listless and tired.

"You've heard from Jensen again," I surmised. "As soon as I dialled, I thought you wouldn't be answering in case it was him."

"Sure, and let him leave something on the machine!"

"Is that what happened?

"You really have to tell Mark now," I said when she didn't respond.

"Remember you promised you wouldn't tell him," Emma said.

"And I'll keep that promise. But you have to tell him."

"I'll figure something out. Don't worry."

"I do worry. How can you say I shouldn't worry?"

"I can deal with it. Everything's going to be all right."

"It doesn't sound that way to me. Just remember I'm here. If you ever need a place to stay, there's room for you. And for Thomas, too. There's the spare room and Thomas can sleep on the couch. Or you can have the couch and Thomas can have the room. And of course, Kelly wouldn't be a problem."

"I don't think it'll come to that."

"Don't tell Mark I told you about that dog. Maybe he'll get Johnny out on bail and he'll be able to look after the dog himself."

Mark was still talking when I carried my tea into the living room.

"It's the only possible explanation," Mark said. "I think I can tell when someone's lying. Hell, I've represented the worst of them and I don't think this kid's lying. He doesn't act like a murderer and he freely admits that he and his father didn't get along. They'd even come to blows once— well, a shoving match is how he put it, but this guy's not the violent type, not one bit. He says he left around six and that his father was, as usual, angry with him. This time he was angry because his room was a mess. The old man's tipped out his dresser drawers before, but Johnny ignored the harangue and got in his van. Stayed the night in Guelph with friends, and went on to

London the next day. He says his father knew he was going to London, which was the real reason for his anger. Johnny's mother lives in London and his father hated her. But his mother wasn't home and Johnny dropped in at a friend's, had a few drinks. It got late and the friend suggested he stay over, but Johnny knew he had to take his father to town the next morning. He didn't think he was over the limit, but he was. And the rest you know."

"The gun could have been planted in Guelph," Marion said.

"In Guelph or in London, even. Especially Guelph. Johnny visits the same people about once a week and often stays over. I'll be talking to these friends— they're musicians, by the way. They've got a group."

"Just like your good old days," I said sarcastically, but Mark was too caught up in his tale to notice.

"Anyway, the van's a mess. Also, the front passenger door doesn't lock any more, but Johnny never bothered to have it fixed because he didn't think it was worth the fuss. He would never have noticed if someone had been in the van."

"I think if the gun was planted it would have been in Guelph," Marion said. "Whoever did it must have known he stayed overnight, whereas in London they wouldn't have known that."

"That's what I think, too," Mark said. "But proving it is something different altogether."

"You'll sound like an idiot if you use the Anastasia connection in court," I said.

"What about lawyer-client confidentiality?" Peter asked. "Should you be telling us all this?"

He yawned theatrically.

"Johnny knows I'm talking to you people. Not to worry. Any coffee left?" Mark asked me.

"I'm for bed," Peter announced curtly.

"Sure, go on to bed if you're tired," Mark said.

Marion jumped up to make more coffee. I followed Peter to the bedroom and sat on the bed while he threw off his clothes.

"Sometimes Mark is just too much," he said, stepping into his pyjama bottoms. He'd been wearing pyjamas since Conrad arrived, so as not to get nipped in vital places. "Doesn't he know it's after one?"

He tossed back the quilt and got into bed. I lay beside him on top of the quilt. Conrad scratched at the door.

"We forgot to take him out," Peter said.

"I'll do it. Then I'll join you in bed."

Marion and Mark had moved to the kitchen and were drinking coffee. They barely acknowledged me as I took Conrad's leash from the hook by the back door and went outside, where Conrad did his business quickly. When I returned, Marion had her Anastasia books on the kitchen table.

I said I was exhausted and went to bed. With a sigh, Conrad settled at my feet. Peter was half asleep, but he reached down, gave his dog a reassuring pat, and put his arm around me.

"So when can we expect her home?"

Hugh on the phone. The clock radio read 9:45. I hadn't even heard Peter leaving and Conrad was, for a change, sleeping soundly at the foot of the bed.

"I don't know, Hugh. Let me get her."

"You sound as if you've just awoken."

"No, I've been up for hours," I lied. "Is anything wrong?"

"Nothing is wrong except Allison has decided she wants to work at the drugstore and she wants her mother to babysit the children after school."

"I'll get Marion."

She was still asleep, but she raised her head when I opened her bedroom door. Her dyed hair stood up in tufts and her eyes looked swollen.

"Umm?"

"Hugh wants to talk to you. Allison wants to work at the drugstore and she wants you to look after the children."

That woke her up. Marion reached for her housecoat and followed me to the kitchen. The coffee cups and glasses hadn't been put in the dishwasher. Mark must have stayed until all hours, I thought. The Anastasia books had slips of paper sticking out of them. At least Peter had made coffee and I poured myself a cup while Marion hummed and hawed on the phone.

At last she said, "I don't know why I should change my plans. Working at the drugstore is hardly an emergency, Hugh, and surely other arrangements can be made for the boys for an hour or two each day. There's Joe's mother and you can keep an eye on them, too."

I passed Marion a cup of coffee.

"I'll be home next week, but tell Allison not to count on me as a regular babysitter... Of course I love those boys... I hardly call working at Roan's Drugstore a career... Tell her to call me then... What? Your good suit is still in the dry-cleaner's bag. In Peter's old room, not in our closet..."

When she hung up, she put her face in her hands.

"Allison can hire a sitter," I said.

"I'll look after them," Marion sighed. "It's all right. And if I have anything on, Hugh will have to pitch in. I just don't like Allison assuming I'll do it. She came over this morning and told Hugh about the job. I can just hear her saying, 'Tell Mom she'll have to come home because I'll be starting work.' The only other job she had was at the dime store, but Joe made her quit that when she became pregnant. Roan's Drugstore! I do wish she'd set her sights a bit higher."

"But there's not much else in Meredith."

"Exactly. She should take a course. When she was a little girl she said she wanted to be a doctor. I'm ashamed to say I told her that women became nurses, not doctors."

"Times change."

"We change, and a good thing it is, too. When I think how rigid we were, in our roles and thinking... Sorry for the mess. Mark stayed until three. I planned to tidy up in the morning before you were up, but I overslept. Too much coffee. I was awake until five."

"Mark certainly likes to talk. He was always that way."

"I think we covered every aspect of Anna Anderson's life after you went to bed. I'm not sure this morning what all that has to do with poor Johnny's situation, but it seemed clear last night."

"I bet he won't use the Anastasia angle in court. It's just a lot of talk."

"I don't know. He's pretty convinced Johnny is innocent and that someone planted the gun. He asked if I'd help him."

"How?"

"Oh, read more books— background information. He's going to call some libraries, find out where we can get some of the out-of-print books." I must have looked incredulous because she admitted this idea did sound ridiculous this morning. "Here a young man has been charged with murder and I'm supposed to read old Romanov books. It does seem like lunacy. And I really should get home to look after my grandkids... But I've been wanting to read those books for a long time."

"I think the whole thing is straight out of the loony bin," I said. "Late night talk. That's Mark. His mouth runs away with him. I don't think he knows what he's saying half the time. Maybe he's not even the best choice for a lawyer for Johnny. And who's going to pay the legal costs?"

It would be just like Mark to take a case for free and to hell with paying the mortgage. I knew Emma and Mark owed a hefty balance on the farm and that Mark's mother, who was loaded, hadn't helped them, although she had been prepared to finance a house when Mark was engaged to the lawyer.

The telephone rang.

"This is Mrs. Carolyn Archer?" The voice was female, strong, with a heavy German accent.

"Speaking."

"This is Tetta Schwartz, the mother of George." She pronounced it the German way. "You have heard of this terrible business?"

"Yes. I'm very sorry for your loss."

"I thank you for your sympathy." The voice didn't break. "It is impossible to talk on the telephone. He said I must speak with you if anything did happen."

"Johnny said you should speak with me?"

"My son, George. You must come to me, the sooner the better."

I didn't like this "must." Her manner reminded me of her son's. I suggested she get in touch with Johnny's lawyer, but she said "Gay-org" had insisted she speak to me.

"We must meet. This is essential."

"I feel as if I'm under orders," I told Marion as we set out for Kitchener to meet Tetta Schwartz. "The woman's son has been murdered and her grandson's been arrested for it, but she seemed so cool. And here I am, obeying her. She sounds unpleasant. And all this cloak and dagger stuff."

We were to meet at the pavilion in Victoria Park in the middle of Kitchener. I had given a talk there for a Culture Fest about Canadian pioneer cooking. That was in the summer when the place was packed, but there wouldn't be many people around on this fall day in the middle of the week, and I decided to take Conrad. I'd keep him on the leash and after our meeting I'd let him loose in the wilder area at the edge of the park. I knew some gay-bashing went on in the park at night, but there shouldn't be any trouble in broad daylight.

There was only one other car in the parking lot of Victoria Park. It was a grey, overcast day and the park was deserted. Conrad's panting as he strained to reach the ducks in the pond was the only sound.

It was a large park, with paths surrounding the central lake and little bridges spanning the water. In the summer kids played at the playground areas, families picnicked, sweethearts walked hand-in-hand, old people sat on benches, and everyone fed the ducks. The trees were huge, the bushes plentiful. Kids have skated on the frozen lake in winter for about a hundred years, and once a bust of Kaiser Wilhelm was toppled into the lake. Kitchener was settled mainly by Germans and was called Berlin until the first world war.

A lone woman in a tweed coat sat on a bench near the pavilion. She didn't stir, nor did she glance up at our approach, although Conrad was barking. She was so erect, so unmoving, that she seemed to be in a sepia photograph.

There was something about her. Even Conrad grew quiet and trotted obediently at my side. At last she looked in our direction. I thought of castles, of coaches and fairy tales, of tea tables in the garden. Of George's ("Gay-org's") living room and the wall unit, the old pictures.

She stood up to shake hands. She was very small, barely five feet, but her bearing was erect. She used no make-up on her soft, lined face and her white hair was fastened into an old-fashioned bun. If she was surprised that I had brought Marion along, she didn't show it.

We sat down. Conrad gave one tentative pull towards the water, then settled down with his head between his paws. Marion was the first to speak, saying how lovely the park was.

"It would have been better to choose another location," Mrs. Schwartz said. "I did not realize we would be so in the open here."

"I didn't see anyone else around," I said. "If someone comes, Conrad will let us know, I'm sure."

Conrad stirred at the sound of his name, but a small "pop" made him quiet again. But a dog hadn't protected George Austin-Wright, I thought.

Mrs. Schwartz reached into her handbag and took out a picture, which she handed over without a word.

It showed a young boy grinning beside Anna Anderson. Although it was obviously summer because the bushes in the background were in bloom, Anna Anderson wore a jacket and had a scarf wrapped around her neck. The boy wore *Lederhosen* and his shirt tail was sticking out.

"My son and Grand Duchess Anastasia," Mrs. Schwartz said. She pronounced "Anastasia" in the European way: Ah-nah-stahsiah.

I heard Marion's in-take of breath as she took the picture from me. Mrs. Schwartz smiled.

"Yes, he told me she'd taught him to ride a bike," I said.

"They were very best friends. He went to her apartment every morning. In and out. She did not like much to be bothered but George was permitted to go in and go out, as if he had been her son."

She stretched her hand out for the picture and Marion reluctantly handed it over.

"She went into the road to teach him to ride the bicycle, and that is a thing she did seldom. Her scarf became caught in the wheels of the bicycle. She allowed George to call her by her first name. He would come home and talk about the picture of Rasputin on her wall, and that of the Tsar. He would have tea with her. Every day after school he would stop first at her apartment and then go to his own... That was on the Johann Trojan Strasse, in the days before our lovely city was destroyed by the English bombers. Many times we sat with the Grand Duchess in the air-raid shelter. My son would cry and Anastasia would tell him stories of her childhood.

"So you see, George knew her very well, very well," she concluded with satisfaction. "To the others she was Her Imperial Highness, but to George she was simply his friend Anastasia. She was not so haughty with my young George, as she was with the others. She was sometimes difficult, even with her closest friends, but after her experiences this was not to be wondered at. The people who owned the newspaper in our city would take her for drives in their big automobile, and even with these she was sometimes not pleasant.

"And later, after the war, when we found her in the Black Forest, she quarrelled with the ladies who looked after her, but she was happy to see my son again. She had big dogs to keep the newspaper reporters away, but even these big beasts knew George was a friend."

I asked Mrs. Schwartz if she had heard about the DNA tests.

"Nonsense," Mrs. Schwartz said. "But I am not surprised. Her enemies would not let her triumph, even after death. To allow the truth to be told now would be to ruin the reputation of these big people. The truth would never be allowed. And now they have killed my son, so he could not tell what he knew."

"But why now?" I asked.

"Because you had seen him about this book. He perhaps told someone of your interest and so they shoot him before he can talk to you. It is very dangerous."

"It's about money, isn't it?"

She nodded. "It is about more money than you can imagine. Fortunes. That is what my son knew. These people shot him."

"Which people?"

"The people who want the money."

"But if Anna Anderson is dead..."

"He knew other things as well. He knew things about Anastasia's enemies. Many, many things. You are a writer of books, and so he would tell you and you would write a book, which is what they did not want."

"And you want me to write this book, even if it's so dangerous?"

"The truth must come out."

But she doesn't care if I die, I thought. Like hell, I told myself.

"You should talk to Johnny's lawyer," I said. "He's the one you should talk to. He's very interested in the Romanov angle."

Her head jerked up. "How do you know this?"

"He's a friend of ours. A good friend. I told him about your son's interest in Anastasia."

"You told this before my son was shot?"

"I believe I mentioned it, yes. Mark's always been interested in Russian history."

Mrs. Schwartz stared at me.

I stared right back.

No one said anything.

I decided to be frank.

"Anna Anderson probably wasn't even Anastasia," I said. "They did two DNA tests on her intestine and one on her hair. Two different teams of scientists concluded she was really Franziska Schanzkowska."

"That is impossible," the old woman said.

"What I find interesting," Marion said, "is if she was indeed Franziska, how she carried it off. Did she really believe she was Anastasia? And how could she convince so many people? If she really was Franziska, I still admire her for rising above her background to such a degree. Of course she still could have been Anastasia. They could have switched samples, for instance."

"Everyone in Hanover knew she was Anastasia!" Mrs. Schwartz' voice rose. "The tests do not convince me because I knew she was Anastasia. My son knew she was Anastasia!"

"I believe she was Franziska," I said.

This was not going well at all. Mrs. Schwartz' face was red.

"If she was Franziska she was still the woman you knew," Marion said softly.

"Never, never, never in a million years! The authorities forced her to meet this peasant family in 1938 and nothing came of it!"

"Mark thinks that even if she was Franziska she could have known things about the money because someone told her," I said, not caring if Mark wanted me to repeat his opinion or not. "I'm beginning to feel so sorry for Anna Anderson, for Franziska. People were only interested in her if she was Anastasia and she knew it. Maybe that's why she was difficult. No one cared about the woman, only about her image."

Mrs. Schwartz stood up and faced us.

Her mouth opened to speak, but she changed her mind, turned on her heel and walked off.

"But— " Marion cried. "Wait, please..."

It was no good. Mrs. Schwartz walked on. She had gone about fifty feet when she tottered and almost fell, but she righted herself without looking back and continued walking. Conrad barked.

I've rarely seen Marion angry, and I've certainly never had cross words with her, but she was definitely annoyed with me as we walked to the end of the park so Conrad could have his run. I was irritated as well, angry at the very idea that this autocratic old woman would expect me to risk my life for her wretched son's honour, and annoyed that Marion was upset that I'd ruined the interview.

We didn't speak until we came to the wooded, untended area, where I let Conrad free.

"That was obviously a waste of time," Marion remarked sourly. "That awful woman."

"And now I'll never know what she knew," Marion said, giving me the kind of look she gives Hugh when she's fed up with him.

"You can always speak to her on your own," I told Marion. "Especially now that you have your own car," I added bitchily.

Chapter Eight

The coolness between Marion and me continued until she left for Meredith two days later. She spoke to Mark by telephone and she took off in her car several times. She didn't tell me what was said or where she went and I didn't ask. I worked on my latest mystery, but it was hard to concentrate. When I found out after her departure that she'd gone to The Bookworm and invited Peter for lunch, I felt as I had with Charlie's mother, who'd been a true bitch.

What I needed was a good gossip, a get-it-off-my-chest session. I called Emma and asked her for lunch at The Bookshelf, a bookshop-cum-trendy cafe in downtown Guelph.

Emma was happier than she'd been for some time. Her eyes were bright and she seemed to glow. The reason for this was that she'd sold three wall hangings the day before. She'd always meant to market them, she said, and Mark was forever encouraging her to do so, but she'd held back, thinking her work wasn't good enough. Yesterday she'd taken them to a craft store, and, surprise, surprise, three of the five had sold that very day.

"It was just a one-time thing," Emma said. "These rich Americans were touring Canada and they saw my hangings and bought them immediately. The other two'll probably be there for years, but it's a start. Mark thinks I should go to craft fairs and art shows."

"It's great. It sounds like everything's happier on the home front."

"Oh, Mark's happy he's working on this murder business. The Romanovs and all. I think maybe he was just getting bored at work, dealing with nothing but real estate and divorce. Here he has this kid who's accused of killing his father he's trying to get bail for and he goes around the house at night whistling all the time. And talking to Marion about the Romanovs. He doesn't even notice what Thomas is doing half the time, which is fine with me."

"And the other thing?"

"I haven't heard anything since I told Jensen we were taking legal action against him for harassment. So I'm hoping that's that."

She sounded a bit too glib for me, too off-hand, but I let it pass. Anyway, I wanted to get Marion off my chest.

"You say Mark talked to Marion for an hour? She must have called from her bedroom. She didn't tell me anything about that."

"Oh, yes, Mark was home part of yesterday afternoon because he visited Johnny in jail. He must have told Marion where he'd be, because he wasn't home fifteen minutes before she called. It was 'Romanov' this and 'Anastasia' that. I'd taken the hangings in that morning and I felt pretty keyed up, so I went outside and cleaned out the flower beds. He was still talking to Marion when I went inside to start dinner. If he'd talked any longer the craft place wouldn't have reached me. But at least it was Marion he was talking to, not his mother."

"Mothers-in-law," I said, and Emma was off, saying that they had been blessed with a visit from Mark's mother on Sunday afternoon. She had pointedly asked several times if the quilts were paying for themselves yet. And then Thomas upset his milk at dinner and it dripped on her dress, which happened to be silk, and panic ensued. Mark ran like mad for a wet cloth, as if he was worried about his mother's dress ("And I bet he was, too!" Emma said) and Mother dear had mentioned Sandra, Mark's ex-fiancee, twice as she was leaving.

"Well, Marion sneaked downtown and took her son out for lunch," I said.

"They probably discussed you," Emma said. "They all want to be together with their sons, without the wife. All men are mama's boys, believe me. Remember long ago? When Mark took his laundry home? Not only was I an immigrant slut, but I didn't have enough brains to launder a shirt. She used to send his t-shirts back ironed, and once he took some tea towels to her by mistake and she ironed them, too. Not only that, but Mark, the Communist, Marxist hippie, pointed that fact out to me. If she had known that Mark and I would eventually marry, I think she would have hired a hit man to do me in."

"Peter didn't even tell me his mother had lunch with him," I said. "It just slipped out because he wasn't very hungry that night. Otherwise I wouldn't have known."

Emma nodded.

"At first Mark's mother wasn't even going to come to the wedding. Did you know that? She said if we couldn't bother doing things properly, she didn't know why she should make an effort. And then she asked who was paying for the wedding, such as it was. She pointed out that it was *traditional* for the bride's family to foot the bill. And she kept getting my mother's name wrong when we went out for dinner afterwards! One good thing, your mother-in-law still has a husband. Mine only has a son. Where did Peter and his mother have lunch?"

"At Swiss Chalet."

"They know you never go to the Swiss Chalet, right? Like a secret date. Do you know another thing that happened when we were first married? His mother invited us to her country club, and before we went she phoned me to tell me not to worry about being nervous, because there were other people in the club who'd come from the wrong side of the tracks, too."

"Did you go to the club?"

"Yup, and when Her Highness introduced me to a friend of hers, this old biddy, I said, 'Hello, I'm Emma, from the wrong side of the tracks.' She was furious, his mother."

"And you've never been back to the club, I bet."

"Never."

"How did Mark react to that— to what you said?"

"Oh, he said it was great and he laughed, but you know what? Underneath I think he was embarrassed."

"I don't believe it."

"Believe me, he was embarrassed. He might still want you to think all his ideals from the sixties are intact, but he's ambitious. I mean, like I said, he even ran for the boring School Board last year."

"Maybe you'll be wife to the Prime Minister."

Emma laughed. "Oh, and speaking of the Board, guess who applied for an electrician's job with the Board? Our doggies' grandpa, Scottie. He called and asked Mark to put in a good word for him."

"There's a mama's boy for you," I said. "Can you imagine having Mabel for a mother-in-law?"

We giggled about that for a while, which in a way was a relief because I was beginning to feel guilty about trashing Marion so mightily. Now that I had voiced my complaints, I felt much better about her. She really was an angel, I told myself, unlike Emma's m-i-l, who truly was a person I didn't like. I'd only met her once, by chance on the street, when Emma and I were shopping. In about five minutes, she got in two digs. She said to Emma, "So this is your clever friend," implying that Emma was anything but clever. And she censored Emma for not waiting for after-Christmas sales, as she had always done.

Emma, feeling rich, insisted on paying our lunch bill. On the way out, I remembered to ask about Mark's nutty plans for Hans.

"Oh, if Johnny doesn't make bail, Scottie and mama will board Hans in their kennel. A little light blackmail. Mark puts in a good word for Scottie and Scottie relieves Mark of that beast!"

"But Mabel hates Hans."

"She'll probably feed him broken glass. Don't forget she's Scottish. Money, money."

That night I prepared a special dinner: baked Camembert to start with, Swiss onion soup, mushroom and chicken ragout, parsley rice, dilled carrots and sugar peas from the freezer, and raspberries for dessert. We don't have a dining room, but the eating area of the kitchen, next to my study, is large, and by the time Peter came home, tired and hungry, I had the table set with my grandmother's pretty hand-painted violet dishes and the pink wine glasses that went with them so well.

"What's this for?" Peter asked, looking at the table.

"I don't know. I just felt like it." I put my arms around him, which of course got Conrad going. We could do anything in bed and Conrad was oblivious, but he became the green-eyed monster when we showed major affection during the day.

"Hmm," Peter said, breathing into my hair and ignoring Conrad, who was trying to get between us. "Does this have anything to do with my mother leaving?"

"Of course not." Conrad thrust his nose between our legs. Peter pushed him away and we ran to the bedroom. Peter slammed the door on a furious dog.

"The food'll get cold," I said, as I unbuttoned my blouse.

"What are microwaves for?" Peter asked.

We were lying there half asleep— and had I turned the burner off beneath the soup? I wondered— when the door bell rang. At the sound, Conrad, who was panting by the bedroom door in a most resentful way, started barking.

"Don't answer it," Peter said. "It's probably Mark with his latest Romanov theory."

The bell rang again, sending Conrad to the front door.

"Maybe it's only a Girl Guide selling cookies," Peter said as I pulled on my jeans. By the time I reached the door, Neil Andersen, in civvies, was just getting into a brown Ford Escort. But he peered over his shoulder and saw me in the open door. He looked sheepish.

"I'm not disturbing you or anything, am I? You look a little sleepy."

"Oh no, I've been cooking, that's all." I know I blushed.

"This isn't anything official," he said.

"Come in anyway."

Peter came out of the bedroom just as Neil stepped into the hall. Now Neil blushed. I could see the relief on Peter's face that our caller wasn't Mark. I introduced them and invited Neil to stay for dinner.

Conrad was barking all through this. It was a good thing Neil didn't have his uniform on. Conrad was still carrying on when Neil sat at the table with a glass of wine. Neil wasn't going to stay, he said, but it was in an unconvincing manner, and I set another place.

"I'm not interrupting a special occasion, am I? Like an anniversary, or something like that?" he asked, looking at the table.

"No, I go on these crazy cooking binges. I'm the cookbook lady when all's said and done."

"It certainly smells good." He sipped his wine. "But I didn't come here expecting to be fed."

"Well, be fed anyway."

He laughed and I poured myself a glass of wine. I had, after all, turned the burner off beneath the soup. The ragout and the Camembert were in the oven and I only had to re-heat the vegetables in the microwave.

I brought the cheese in its brown crust to the table, along with a small glass dish of currant jelly.

"We can nibble on this while we wait for Peter," I said.

"What is it?"

"Baked Camembert. Melted cheese in pastry."

"Something new for me," he said, taking a slice as Peter, freshly showered, came into the kitchen. "I grew up on meat and potatoes, real Prairie kid, and when I got married it was more meat and potatoes, although of the frozen food variety. Lucky guy," he said to Peter.

"He's a regular chauvinist," I said. "I do almost all the cooking around here."

"That's because I'd never come up to scratch," Peter said. "And anyway, you like to cook."

That was true. I did like to cook, and when it came to the kitchen I was pretty chauvinistic myself. I hated the messes when Peter cooked, the bland taste of the food.

I knew I was showing off for Neil. And glad his wife couldn't cook.

Neil waited until we were through the soup before telling us the reason for his visit.

"This is not what a good police officer is supposed to do," he said, "but after we talked about the Romanovs and Anastasia, I got to thinking about this old Russian guy back home."

Peter sighed. (Not him, too!)

"You know, out west we have all kinds of Russians, but they're mostly Ukrainians. This fellow was from Siberia, a real Russki, as he was called. He had a shoe repair shop, and he was ugly as sin, scary, too, a tiny shrivelled up old guy with a wife who looked just like him. We used to run by his place screaming 'Witch! Witch!' if he wasn't home. He used to go out to the country, selling shoes and such. We didn't dare try our shenanigans when the old guy was home— we were all afraid of him.

"Anyway, anyway— is this chicken? does it ever smell good—

one time when I was alone I screamed out 'Witch' and the old guy was there after all, and he grabbed me. I guess I didn't see his truck because this time he had it parked behind the cabbage patch.

"Well, he grabbed me by my collar and lectured me about not having manners and told me that one day I would be old, too, as old as him and his wife, which was a pretty scary thing to say to a kid. Naturally I didn't believe him, not when he said it, and I laughed, and then he pushed me into his truck and drove me home.

"My mother, of course, was mortified, and the next day she came with me when I apologized to the old woman, who didn't understand a single word I said. She gave my mother a cabbage, I remember.

"But here's the remarkable thing. That night my mother sat me down and told me that this man, this old shoemaker, had known the Tsar of Russia in Siberia. Guarded him or something, I can't be sure. Maybe he'd been a servant. Most of it went over my head, but it came back when you talked about Anastasia. I thought I remembered my mother also saying that this man had said Anastasia escaped. I couldn't remember for sure, so I didn't say anything until I checked with her.

"And guess what? He did say that Anastasia survived. My mother was so interested, this was about the time of the movie with Ingrid Bergman, that she wrote down what he said.

"But here's the most interesting part. This old guy's still alive, in the nursing home. They recently had a hundred year birthday party for him. My mother's going to visit him and see if he knows anything else. Apparently his memory's still good. If he knows anything he'll tell my mother because she became pretty friendly with his wife after my bad behaviour. My mother would bring her pies and cakes, and bread, soft white Canadian bread because the old woman had no teeth and couldn't chew very well. The old lady would give her things from her garden."

He looked at us, pleased with himself.

"I wish my mother-in-law were still here, because she's the one who's really interested in Anastasia," I said. Neil looked disappointed, and because of this I found myself telling him about our meeting with Austin-Wright's mother.

"So you see, there are people who think his death is the result of some kind of secret political cabal."

Neil shook his head. I knew he couldn't— wouldn't— tell me much because the investigation was still going on.

"I say the son finally lost it with the old man," Peter said. "Just another domestic tragedy, like the ones my father was always being called out for in Meredith. People hold grudges, tempers flare, anger simmers, and then, one day, whammo. Add some alcohol, put in a gun that's lying around. Dogpatch city."

"You don't need dogpatch for domestics," Neil remarked.

"That old Austin-Wright guy seemed like a jerk to me when I met him at Oktoberfest. Crying in his beer. I bet he was a bugger to live with. He probably went too far and the son snapped," Peter said.

Neil didn't comment on this.

After Neil left, Peter stacked the dishwasher; I took a cup of coffee into the living room and put on a Chopin CD. The light music wasn't soothing. I felt restless, keyed up. All the talk about domestic violence made me think of Emma and Mark and that Jensen character. I kept thinking of Mark with his tie off, talking and talking with Marion in the kitchen that night. How innocent he'd sounded, spinning historical theories. Kings and queens and lost princesses, and now Neil, in what had to be a totally unusual action for a professional police officer, had contacted his mother on the prairies about some long-forgotten character who had known about the Tsar's execution. There was magic in royalty.

But the magic was deceptive. Nero fiddled while Rome burned, and Tsar Nicholas remained isolated with his family while his empire fell apart. The Russian royal family were killed by the Bolsheviks and here, today, we were still feeling reverberations and dipping into the mystery of Anastasia, whose story still was more compelling than the possibility of an "ordinary" murder.

"Dishes done," Peter said. He had a towel wrapped around his middle and carried a half-full bottle of wine and two glasses. He poured two glasses and sat beside me on the couch.

"Good meal," he said. "You outdid yourself. The cop appreciated it, too."

"I'm glad there was enough to go around."

"Amazing, isn't it, that he'd call his mother to find out about this old Russian guy, and then come over here to tell us about it?"

"He probably smelled the food cooking."

"I'm glad my mother wasn't here. They'd still be gabbing away."

"I wish George had been killed because of what he knew about Anna Anderson," I said. I drained the wine. It tasted bitter, vinegary. "Instead of by his son in a dirty little squabble. I hope Johnny didn't do it."

"Maybe he can plead self-defence. Maybe he was provoked. Maybe George had the gun and one thing led to another. It wouldn't be a planned murder. It's true he took off, but who wouldn't? He should have taken the dog away with him. The dog was a dead giveaway because no one else could have gotten past the dog. But I guess he wasn't thinking too clearly. Shouldn't we be hitting the sack?"

"I don't know if I can sleep or not. Too much coffee late at night. Maybe I'll take Conrad out for a walk. Want to come?"

I'd said the wrong words. "Walk" brought Conrad, who'd been asleep at the end of the couch, to full alertness, and he started barking at me.

"You take him," Peter said above the racket. "I'll go to bed and read."

One good thing about having Conrad was that I didn't have to be afraid of getting mugged or raped. Women and kids could come up to him and pat him and he glowed in the attention, but let a man approach me, even to say "Nice day," and Conrad growled and bared his teeth. I was his woman and he wasn't going to let any strange male forget it.

It was chilly, with that autumn tang in the air. Our neighbourhood's pretty safe, but I hadn't walked alone at night until we got Conrad.

"Heel, Conrad, heel." He wasn't really straining that hard, but the words reassured me. The words and the leash and the animal at the end of the leash were comforting.

We made our way to the end of the street. Conrad stopped to piddle at three fence posts, a fire hydrant and some driftwood positioned in a rock garden next to the sidewalk. When I tugged at the leash to pivot him around, he pulled the other way.

"What? You're not sleepy yet either?" His tongue stuck out in that lopsided grin that always got to me. "You don't want to go home yet? All right, you're the boss."

I really wanted to go home. I was getting colder by the minute— it was much damper out than I'd supposed and I wished I'd worn my parka. On the other hand, Conrad was having fun. Part of Peter's logic for getting a dog had been that we would have to walk him and therefore be forced to get needed exercise.

Away from our familiar street, Conrad tugged harder, as if the freedom from routine granted him additional privileges. I'd never taken him this far at night, and as we turned towards downtown, he lunged ahead, panting and choking as I tried to "pop" the choker.

"No, Conrad, no!" But he was determined to forge ahead and I knew where he was taking me: to the school grounds where we had let him run off the leash in the summer.

In the school yard, I slipped off the choker and Conrad was off like a shot, circling around the trees, stopping to sniff something in the grass and to pee on a tree, but always looking back to see where I was. I knew if I cried out he'd be right back. I wished I had a ball with me to throw, although Conrad still didn't understand that he had to drop it. I picked up a piece of wood and threw that. Maybe the action would warm me up.

"Fetch— c'mon, boy!"

The wood sailed past him, but he didn't react. He was eating something, I saw as I approached, and he wasn't going to let me have it.

"No! Conrad! No!" I yelled.

But he wouldn't release the object, which turned out to be a baggie containing what looked like a sandwich.

"No! Drop it! Leave it!" *Leave it* was the term we used in Puppy Kindergarten, where Conrad, under Hitler's eyes, had successfully dropped a red ball more than once. Alas, Hitler wasn't here and Conrad knew he didn't have to release his evening snack. He allowed me to slip the choker over his head and even gave a tentative wag of the tail, but his jaws remained clamped shut.

I dragged him to the sidewalk where it was easier to see in the light of the street lamp.

"No! No! Leave it!" Pop! Pop! Pop!

I rolled him over on his back and sat on him. In this submissive position, with his neck bared, he allowed me to pry his mouth open. I grasped the end of the baggie. He could have bitten me easily enough, but he didn't. Instead his throat worked convulsively as he tried to swallow. His brown eyes regarded me with a quizzical look: I didn't understand! The sandwich was his, manna from heaven, and he was going to eat it!

I gripped harder and I think I would have had the baggie out from between his teeth, if a vehicle hadn't stopped. A familiar voice asked, "What's this now?" Conrad recognized Scottie's voice and struggled to get up, but I held him down, still straddling him, and looked over my shoulder to see Scottie leaning out of his truck window.

The baggie disappeared down Conrad's gullet.

Scottie jumped out of the truck and Conrad barrelled over, barking and jumping.

"He found some kid's lunch and swallowed it, plastic bag and the works! What if there's broken glass in there, or drugs?" We'd had stern lectures at Puppy Kindergarten about the importance of seeing that dogs did not swallow foreign objects, which could lodge in the intestine and require dangerous and expensive surgery. Dogs could die if they swallowed nails.

"Sit, boy, sit, that's it." Scottie snapped his fingers. Miraculously, Conrad sat.

"I couldn't get it away from him," I explained. "He let me put my hand down his throat and he just kept swallowing. Should I take him to the emergency vet clinic?"

Scottie regarded Conrad.

"A plastic bag, you say? Likely as not it'll pass through him. Unless there's bones in there, which is hardly likely, I'd say he'll be fine. And I wouldn't worry about drugs. What mother would pack a lunch with drugs, I ask you? And what kid would throw the drugs away if she did?"

Scottie chuckled. I smelled whiskey on his breath.

"Come on, I'll give you and the pup a drive home." He patted Conrad's head, which Conrad saw as permission to get up. "Sit, Conrad." Conrad sat. Scottie reached for the leash. "Mother's not along, so there'll be plenty of room."

Conrad, glancing at Scottie, soon settled at my feet. I was glad of the truck's warmth, but Scottie's whiskey breath was stronger than it had been in the open air. I could smell something else too—after-shave, I thought.

"You're out late," I told Scottie.

"Whist. Over at the union hall," Scottie said happily, starting the engine. "Lancaster, isn't it?"

Scottie had never been to our house, but we'd discussed Guelph neighbourhoods.

"You really didn't have to give me a ride home," I said.

"Ah, no," Scottie said, "it's late and it's hardly out of my way at all. I was taking a spin anyway."

"Your mother didn't join you at cards?" I knew Mabel and Scottie often went out to play cards at the union hall and in church basements.

"She does like her cards, but she felt a cold coming on tonight." Scottie grinned. He didn't appear unhappy to be out alone. "Conrad's quite the lamb now," he remarked.

"I don't know. He knows he can get away with murder with me. I should have been able to get that sandwich away from him," I sighed.

"Bring him 'round home," Scottie said. "I'll have a go with him."

"I wouldn't want to put you to any trouble."

"No trouble," Scottie said, and launched into a tale of Lady's puppyhood, when he and Mabel still lived in a duplex apartment. Lady had chewed slippers and shoes, but her sins were white compared to the misdeeds of young Labradors, who generally loved anything that went into their mouths.

I didn't bring up Johnny and neither did he, although I knew he must have heard.

"Now you come out and let me have a session with the young whipper-snapper," Scottie said as he dropped us off.

"Thanks. I'll call first. But I really don't want to put you to trouble."

"You wouldn't by any chance play cards yourself?" Scottie asked.

"Bridge, but not well. We've played with Peter's parents."

"There you go then. I'll trade you a training session with young Conrad and you and your husband have a game with us. Mother would be delighted to have you. Nothing like a game of cards. There's no better pastime. Cards and some lunch makes for a fine evening."

Letting us off, Scottie called out, "Toodley-do, then!"

The next morning, Conrad passed the baggie, which contained a perfect egg salad sandwich.

Chapter Nine

Johnny Austin-Wright made bail two days later, the $100,000 bond posted by his mother, Marlies, who had used her house in London as surety. Mark dropped in to tell me.

"A tough nut to crack," Mark told me. "I couldn't make her see that it wouldn't do any good for Johnny to rot in jail until the trial gets underway. She had to convince her husband, too, who thinks Johnny's nothing but a no-good doper."

"Is he?"

"The cops didn't find anything in his possession and there weren't any interesting weeds growing at the nursery."

"The thought occurred to you?"

"Sure, but pot's Mickey Mouse, always has been unless you grow enough to sell. But they didn't find anything."

Did Mark still smoke pot? I wondered. Emma had never said and we'd never been offered any, but I could believe Mark would have his own interesting weed growing on that hobby farm of his. If so, I hoped it was well hidden. Pot wouldn't do his image as the burgeoning politician any good.

"So what's this Marlies like?" I couldn't imagine anyone married to George.

"Blonde, Teutonic. She reminds me of Marlene Dietrich. Guess what business she and her hubby are in?"

I shook my head.

"The nursery business, just like your buddy George! The husband's Dutch, they have all these windmills around the shop and specialize in bulbs from Holland. The husband wouldn't put up the business— nothing doing— but Marlene Dietrich's name is on the deed to the house, and she finally talked him into it. I tried to make her take Johnny into her home, but that was a no-go. Hubby won't have him around and Johnny wasn't keen anyway. Doesn't get along with the step-father, got thrown out of the house four years ago when he was eighteen and hightailed it back to Father George."

"Why did he get thrown out?"

"Jan, the husband, said Johnny threatened him. Jan's super-straight, a hard worker, came to Canada with nothing. Built up the business. Widower, met Marlies, who was selling real estate in London. He says Johnny's just like his father."

"Do they think Johnny killed his father?"

"Jan does. The mother won't say, but I bet her husband wants Johnny to be guilty to get him out of the way. Apparently it was a very bitter divorce and George never paid Marlies everything he was supposed to."

"What does Marlies say about George?"

"Won't talk about him, except to say that he was crazy. That's where you come in."

"Me? What for?"

"I thought you could talk to her, find out everything you can."

"I thought Marion was going to be your little handmaiden."

"But Marion's back in Meredith."

"I didn't do so well with George's mother, but I guess Marion already told you that."

Mark spread his hands.

"Why don't you ask Emma to go to London with you? I'll look after Thomas after school."

"Emma?"

"Why not?"

"She doesn't have the interest."

"Of course Emma's interested in what you do."

"I mean interest in the Romanovs. I thought you could pay a visit to Marlies from that angle. You know, see what she knows about Anna Anderson and kind of lead into the marital history."

"This is nuts. You still want to pursue this Romanov business?"

"Johnny did not kill his father. He swears he didn't and I believe him. There's a whole lot more to this than meets the eye. Believe me. Someone planted that gun. Someone had it in for George Austin-Wright and what better person to pin it on than George's own son? If you're not interested in the Romanov angle, how about thinking of helping Johnny? The only way to do that is to find out all we can."

"I honestly do not believe that George's death had anything to do with the Romanovs."

"What else is there?"

"An eccentric, authoritarian man like that could have had a lot of enemies. Business people, someone he insulted... I don't know. As much as I liked Johnny when I met him, it's possible he did his father in. And don't forget the dog. Where's Hans now?"

"Back home. Johnny got him out of doggie hell."

"They're both back at the nursery?"

"Where else? I didn't want him staying with his friends in Guelph. They're kind of weird and since the cops'll be watching him, he's better off at home."

"Ready and waiting for the Romanov agents? I'm surprised you didn't invite him to stay at your place."

"I thought of it, but I didn't think Emma would be too keen. She's busy with her hangings, which is a good thing. She was kind of down in the dumps for a while. Maybe it wasn't such a good idea moving out to the country. Alone too much, and with Thomas at school, I think time was getting pretty heavy. But selling the hangings made a big difference. So how about it? Can I count on you to visit Marlies?"

"Let me think about it."

"Tell you what. Why don't you go and pay Johnny a visit and see how you feel then? You can discuss things with him and then make up your mind."

"Is there going to be a funeral for George?"

"Cremation, no service."

"Nothing? There's going to be nothing?"

"It's what his mother wants, what he wanted apparently. So how about it?"

"I don't really want to get involved, Mark."

"But you are involved. You had an appointment with Johnny's father that night and you and Marion found his body. Let me set something up with Marlies. I told her I knew someone who wanted to write a book about Anastasia and she seemed interested."

Johnny grabbed Hans' collar as I got out of the car. Hans' eyes gleamed and he strained, but he remained obediently at Johnny's side. Conrad, naturally, went wild. I closed the car door.

"Don't worry about Hans," Johnny told me. "Part of the reason he's so nuts is he's been chained up too much. He really won't hurt you. Hold out your hand so he can sniff it."

Eat it, you mean, I thought, but I held my hand out as directed. I don't think I would have in the pre-Conrad era, but I'd learned a little bit about dogs, and I held my hand palm up. Hans sniffed, and then his eyes shifted to mine. For a second our eyes met, his appraising, deep, and I thought, somehow beaten. What did he know, this dog? He could never tell.

"He likes to get his ears rubbed," Johnny said. "Do it and he'll be your buddy for life."

Tentatively, I reached out. Hans snarled and I quickly drew my hand back. "Hans!" Johnny protested, and he stroked the dog's ears.

"Let's go inside," he said. "I could use some coffee."

"Not much business, I take it."

"Nah." He waved an arm dismissively. "I don't think anyone knows we're open," he said, holding the door ajar for me. "Not that we ever exactly did a booming trade."

I stepped over the space where George's body had been. There were no blood stains. Johnny let Hans go.

"Don't worry. Just leave him. He'll get used to you. I've got to get him used to more people. He's really not a bad dog, no matter what anyone says."

"How was he at the Humane Society?" I kept an eye on Hans, who regarded me warily as I followed Johnny to the back of the house. He opened a door and we were in the kitchen.

"Terrified. But who wouldn't be when they're behind bars?" he asked pointedly. Hans settled beneath the table, but he kept his eyes on me.

The room was plain, utilitarian, with faded yellow walls. The uncurtained window looked over fields. Fridge, stove, wooden table with blue chairs that had belonged to a fifties chrome set. There weren't any dishes in the sink and the stove was clean.

"Melitta okay?"

"Wonderful. You must be glad to be back home."

"This looked pretty decent from the other side of the bars, I can tell you that."

Deftly, he spooned coffee into the filter. His shoulders were thin and bony. Innocent.

He poured the hot water into the cone and sat down at the table. His blue eyes were framed by long, sandy eyelashes. I dropped my eyes, and to have something to say, I commented that the house didn't appear to be disturbed. Surely they had dusted it for prints and so on?

Johnny nodded. Mark had hired someone to clean up when the cops were through with the place.

"He's quite the guy, Mark. I used to know him long ago, way before he was a lawyer. He lived on a commune, a real hippie," I told Johnny.

"Yeah, he told me. A real commune with goats. Wanted to be a singer. That coffee should be done." He reached into the cupboard beside the window and took out two white mugs.

"I would never have dreamed back then that Mark would become a lawyer, but I guess in retrospect I'm not surprised. His father was a well-known lawyer, and Mark was always political."

"I guess he couldn't go on raising goats forever," Johnny said. He poured milk into a glass pitcher and set out a ceramic jar of sugar cubes. He found tiny silver tongs in a drawer. His father's European ways had rubbed off on him, I thought. "Lots of people have dreams of being musicians."

"What about you?"

"Me? I'm no musician. Most of my friends are into music, but I have no illusions on that score. No pun intended. This may sound nuts to you, but I'm actually looking forward to running the nursery on my own. I could never make a go of it with my father. He scared the customers away. He wasn't the friendliest person in the world. It was either his way or no way at all, and he didn't want to put any money into the business, advertise and so on. Or get in all those extras the other nurseries have. Garden ornaments, Christmas decorations, that kind of stuff."

These were not sentiments he should be voicing, I thought, but would he say these things if he really had killed his father? On the other hand, Mark had told him I would be visiting, and perhaps he felt he could be honest with me.

"I learned a lot from my step-father's business," Johnny said. "I didn't get along with him too well, but I did learn something."

"You told me you write poetry."

He shrugged. Lots of people wrote poetry, he said, but he knew he couldn't make a living that way. He didn't take his poetry seriously, and anyway, he didn't think he had that much talent. He didn't want to be like those people whose handful of poems made them think they were Shakespeare.

We discussed poetry for a while, talked about submitting poems to literary journals and about poetry readings. He went to readings a lot, he said, around Guelph. A friend of his had started a magazine, *Lotus*. Maybe he'd send them something...

I told him I'd met his grandmother.

"She seems to think your father was killed by an agent of the Romanovs, or by someone connected to Anna Anderson's story."

"She and Dad were both on the same wavelength. Mark's barking up that tree, too, but I don't know. A few weeks ago, I would have said it was nuts, Romanov agents— someone connected with them— killing Dad. But I don't know now. I really don't. Someone planted that gun in the van."

"Do you see much of your grandmother?"

"I saw a lot of her as a little kid. Hell, she lived with us for a while, but that was when I was pretty young, three or four, and I really don't remember that much. Oma, that's German for Grandma, and my mother didn't get along, and after I moved to London with my mother, after my parents split up, I saw her maybe two or three times a year. At Christmas, and when I spent a month with my father in the summer. Since I moved back to my father's, we used to see her on Sundays. I'd go and pick her up and she'd spend the day with us. Bring a cake, one of those European things with whipping cream. I'd have coffee with them and disappear. They were always talking about the old days in Germany, raking over the past. I didn't pay that much attention to anything they said. I didn't know the people they were talking about."

"Anna Anderson," I said.

"Yeah. But like I said, it went in one ear and out the other. I used to think it was all nuts, but now I really don't know. On the other hand, my father was the kind of man who made enemies."

"What kind of enemies?"

"Oh, people he felt had stained his honour. He'd write them letters and threaten to sue. That kind of thing. I gave Mark some names."

"What about Hans?" I asked. I'd almost forgotten about the dog, who was resting quietly at Johnny's feet, but watching me.

"Hans would have known some of them. Some of them started as friends. You know, they'd hoist a cool one for the Fatherland and so on, but something always went wrong. I can't give you too many details. I stayed clear of them for the most part, did my own thing. Sometimes Dad would holler down and I'd have to bring up more beer or something."

"Did they argue about women, perhaps?"

"My father was pretty much a monk after my mother left. I doubt if that's how he wanted it. He'd meet these women at some German do but none of them stuck around. He didn't have any women here while I was living with him, that's all I know. He was a real chauvinist of the old school. My mother used to have to polish his shoes and he'd fly in a rage if they weren't done right."

"At least you didn't have to polish his shoes."

"I did, as a kid. But my mother'd do them most of the time."

"He really doesn't sound like a very nice man."

"You've got it."

"But I'm sorry he's dead."

"You know what?" Johnny looked me right in the eye. "I'm sorry he was killed, too. It's hard to describe. He was a real bastard and unless they get me for shooting him, which I can assure you I did not do, my life will be much better without him. But I miss him. Isn't that crazy? He was my father and I do miss him."

"I think that's natural."

"Blood being thicker than water," Johnny said. "It's not something I believed in before. It's even a stupid saying, like something the Nazis would say. You know my father's father was English?"

"Yes. Of course. With a name like Austin-Wright it was perfectly obvious."

"I always wanted to find out about that side of the family, but Oma wouldn't tell me anything. She said if I loved her, I wouldn't try to contact what she called her enemy."

"How about your father? How did he feel?"

"The same as Oma. He hated the English anyway. Detested them."

"The first time I met your father I thought he looked just like Nicholas II. He cried when I told him that."

"That was at Oktoberfest, right?"

I nodded.

"He often cried when he was drunk and talking about the golden past."

"I had this crazy thought he was really Anna Anderson's son."

"No way. Oma's talked about when he was born in the winter and how her sister wrote letters to the husband in England and even telegrammed, but there was no reply. And I don't think Anna Anderson was living in Hanover at the time. He was born in 1929."

"I think Anna Anderson was still in the States then. She went over there to live with Anastasia's cousin, Princess Xenia, but that didn't work out, and she spent a year or two in a clinic before they shipped her back to Germany."

"I really don't know much about her life. I never took much of an interest. It was just another one of his stories. Maybe one day I'll regret not listening."

"Mark wants me to visit your mother," I told him. "Maybe he told you. I said I'd go after I talked to you."

"You wanted to assure yourself I didn't do my father in," he said.

"Yes. That's right."

"So you'll visit my mother?"

"Yes, I've made up my mind."

Unspoken was the question whether I believed that he had killed his father or not.

"She's all right, Mum. When you get to know her. But I can't stand her husband."

"You haven't had much luck with fathers and step-fathers."

"At least they've killed any chauvinistic attitudes I might have had."

"Why don't you try and find some of your English relatives?"

"Maybe I will."

It was time to go. Hans sprang up when I did. Johnny opened the fridge and took out a piece of beef jerky, which he handed to me.

"Tell him to sit."

But Hans wouldn't obey me, or take the treat from my hand. I gave it back to Johnny.

Hans not only sat, but begged like a poodle.

"Oma taught him that," Johnny said.

I decided to drop in on Mabel. Her hawk's eye would have seen my car anyway.

I found her bringing in the wash. She paused, with Scottie's voluminous blue boxer shorts in her hand. I let Conrad out of the car, and Lady unfolded herself from the back step to play with him. They were soon joined by Conrad's parents, whom Conrad greeted with yelps of joy.

"I just wanted to thank Scottie for giving me and Conrad a ride the other night. I guess he's working today."

Mabel nodded. "Thank goodness for that. He's not getting much work these days, but he does what he can." She sighed and put the blue shorts into the basket. They still looked damp to me. It was really getting chilly and I wondered why she bothered to hang the laundry out at all. "He goes when the union tells him to do so, which is not often. Humphrey tells me he has invited you and your husband for a game of cards."

"I was wondering if next Wednesday would be all right."

"I don't think Humphrey has a meeting that night. That will be all right, then."

"I just dropped in to see Johnny."

"You did, did you? The poor lad, that it's come to this. But it's like with a dog. He will take only so much." She felt the waist of a pair of Scottie's green work pants. She frowned and added them to the basket.

"Still hanging clothes out in October," I said conversationally.

"It saves on the electricity bill," she said. "I finish drying them off inside if they're damp. Humphrey likes his clothes to dry in the fresh air."

I told her that Hans was home, too. But she already knew that. She'd seen Johnny with Hans in the van.

"The pair of them had better enjoy their freedom while it lasts," she said. "I certainly do not approve of murder and the boy has never been the ambitious sort, but I'd say he was driven to it."

"You really think he did it?"

"Yes, I do."

She pressed her lips together and turned away to look at the dogs. Conrad seemed to be the lynch pin, falling repeatedly into the play-with-me posture while his parents circled around him. One would dash off and Conrad would follow. Poor Lady did her best to keep up, barking happily at the rear, but it was clear Conrad preferred his own kin.

Mabel's eyes softened as she watched this picture and a smile formed on her lips. It would be a shame, she said, if Conrad ate a poisonous substance. Humphrey would soon teach him, she added, calling the dogs over. The labs came at once, but Lady, as if to make up for lost opportunity, chased Conrad around the field again before coming to heel.

Mabel balanced the laundry basket against her hip, and stroked Lady's ears. With the fall wind whipping Mabel's salt-and-pepper hair around her bony face, it was a scene right out of the Highlands, I imagined.

The problem with my going to London was what to do with Conrad. I'd have to leave him alone all of the next day, and even though Peter could come home for lunch, there'd be all those hours when he could shred carpets and shoes. I called Emma. I'd see her in the evening at Puppy Kindergarten, but I didn't want to leave Conrad's fate to the last minute.

"Sure, drop Conrad off. I'm not going anywhere. I've had a touch of the flu, back and forth to the john a hundred times a day.

Actually, I was going to ask if you could take Thomas and Kelly to obedience classes tonight. Mark has a meeting and he could drop Thomas and Kelly off at your place. You could bring Conrad back and he could stay overnight."

"No problem. Are you okay, Emma?"

"Just the flu."

"Maybe it's stress. If you're worried..."

"No, no. I don't think I'll hear from a certain person again. I don't even want to say his name. That's in the past."

"Maybe the stress has caught up with you."

"No, it's the flu all right. I've got a bit of fever, too. It's going around. Whenever I get the flu it goes straight to my guts."

"Well, it's certainly no problem taking Thomas and Kelly. One of us can keep Conrad in the front and Thomas can restrain Kelly in the back seat. But if you're ill I don't want to burden you with an extra dog."

"I'll throw them out if they get too much. I'll try and watch that Conrad doesn't eat any wood. Thomas can keep an eye on them after school."

"Don't worry about the wood. Conrad'll just throw it up. At least there's nothing else he can eat there." I told her about the baggie incident and that Scottie was going to have a session with Conrad about eating things he found.

But Emma had to excuse herself; she was going to be sick, she said.

Mark dropped Thomas and Kelly off at six-thirty. He didn't have much time. He was on the way to a School Board meeting (applications for the electrician's position were to be reviewed for a short list of people to be interviewed; he'd make sure Scottie would be on the short list, he said), but he was delighted that I'd visited Johnny and would be seeing Marlies the next day.

"I really appreciate it," he said at the door. "I knew you'd come around to share my opinion about Johnny."

"I don't know how I feel about Johnny," I said. I didn't. In Johnny's presence I'd been sure he was innocent, but logically it made sense that he had killed his father. "I'm just going to London tomorrow as a favour to you."

He waved and drove off.

I drove to obedience school. We started off with Peter holding Conrad, and Thomas grasping Kelly in the back, but by the time we came to the end of our street, Peter threw a frantic Conrad into the back seat, where he and Kelly proceeded to step all over Thomas in their joy at being re-united. Another stop. Thomas joined us in the front seat.

"My father says Conrad is much worse than Kelly," he remarked happily.

"Does he now?" Peter asked. He was in a lousy mood because I was going to London tomorrow to see Johnny's mother.

"He says Kelly's smarter than Conrad," Thomas continued self-importantly.

"What do you think?" I asked Thomas.

"Dad just thinks that because I taught Kelly all these things. I bet I could teach them to Conrad, too."

"Maybe you can teach Conrad tomorrow after school. He'll still be there."

"Kelly will get jealous. She sleeps with me, y'know. But Conrad'll be okay in the living room on the rug. That's because he's the alpha male. He'll think he's guarding the pack. The alpha male always sleeps apart in the wild, like with wolves."

"I didn't know that."

"I know that," Peter said testily. "And males are livelier, more independent than females. That's why Conrad's harder to train," he told Thomas pointedly.

What was he doing, arguing with a little boy? I gave him a sharp look, but he turned away.

We didn't even have time to grab our dogs. As soon as Peter opened the car door, they were gone, racing all over the parking lot, chasing each other and barking. "Come, Conrad, come!" Peter yelled, but it did no good. Thomas wouldn't call Kelly at all, saying it was no good to give a command you knew a dog wouldn't obey. Instead he began walking to the door, and as soon as Kelly saw him doing this, she trotted over, although Conrad tried his best to hold her back, running around her in circles and trying to jump on her back.

This gave Peter the opportunity to grab the lead, but Conrad veered the other way, jumping and bumping into Peter's chest. Peter fell down and dropped the leash. Conrad raced after his sister into the building.

"Are you okay?" I bent to help Peter up, but he waved me away and staggered to his feet.

"That damn dog! I knew we couldn't handle both of them. I don't know why you told Emma we'd take Thomas and Kelly tonight." He brushed his knees off and looked over his shoulder. He grimaced. His seat was wet. He'd fallen into a puddle of oil or grease. "Hell! I'll have to go home and change!"

I inspected the damage. Most of his seat was coated with a thick, tar-like substance.

"I'll be back by the time the class is over," he muttered.

Inside the auditorium, Betty had secured Conrad and he sat at her side. Pleased with himself, he grinned up at me, his pink tongue lolling: Look at me, Ma!

Having trashed mothers-in-law, I was hoping to have a tete-a-tete about husbands ("Men! Sometimes I wish Peter...") but Emma, wearing old flannelette pyjamas, was wan and pale when I delivered

Thomas and the dogs. She offered coffee, but I could see she wasn't up to gabbing.

Lying in bed later, there was no puppy breathing at the foot, no furry head to stroke.

"Do you miss him?" Peter asked.

"Yes. Do you?"

"Yes."

"As awful as he is," I said. "I wonder how he's doing?"

"We could call," Peter said.

"It's awfully late."

"Mark'll still be up after his meeting."

"Should I call?"

"I will," Peter decided. "I'll only let it ring once or twice."

I thought of Jensen. Emma would think it was Jensen if the phone only rang a few times. But Emma answered at once, saying Mark wasn't home yet and that Conrad was asleep on her bed.

Chapter Ten

In the morning, the car would not start. The battery? Fan belt? Peter solved the problem when he noticed a puddle of water under the right front wheel: the water pump was leaking. The car would have to go into the shop.

There was just time to catch the Toronto-London train at the Guelph train station. I hadn't relished the thought of the two-and-a-half hour drive on the 401 with its tractor-trailer trucks either returning from the States or going there, to cross at Windsor. The scenery is prettier from the train, too, passing through southern Ontario farm country and small towns which always seem diminished when seen from a four-lane highway. I liked seeing the small, old-fashioned railway stations in Stratford and St. Mary's, barns and tractors, clotheslines and woodsheds from the train window.

The trouble was that, in the muddle over the car, I had forgotten to take a book along. There hadn't been time to buy a paper at the station, and what was I to do with myself? I even read in the car if someone else is driving; I keep a few secondhand paperbacks under the front seat in case of emergency (a tie-up on the highway, for instance). Across the aisle a stout woman wearing a purple sweater was reading a thick Judith Krantz novel and two seats down a bald man was bent over *Bonfire of the Vanities*.

I gazed out of the train window. Without a book to divert me, the barns and country roads seemed boring. I closed my eyes and tried to think about the mystery I had started, the story of the stalked woman set partly in a bed-and-breakfast very much like Marion's and Hugh's, but I fell asleep just before Stratford. By the time the conductor's announcement of "London in five minutes" came, people were already lining up in the aisles with their overnight luggage and the train was passing the disorderly back yards of London's east end.

Groggy, with a bad taste in my mouth, I decided to walk the few blocks to La Galleria, London's downtown shopping mall. I knew that I could walk through the mall and come out a few city blocks away, emerging on Dundas to find: a bookstore! And badly needed coffee in a nearby restaurant.

It was only eleven o'clock. My appointment with Marlies wasn't until one-thirty. Walking through the mall, I found a Cole's book-store and bought a *New Yorker*. The *Globe & Mail* was next, and I might have gone straight for coffee at Say Cheese, the restaurant where I'd eaten when I'd come to London to give a reading, but the bookstore next door had a stack of *The Rain Ascends* by Joy Kogawa in the window.

I couldn't resist temptation. I knew Peter carried the same book at The Bookworm, but I'd put off buying a copy because I hinted it would make a good Christmas present. Well, in this instance, Christmas could come early, I decided, and I nipped into the store. Five minutes later, I had a paid copy under my arm.

You'd think with a bookstore in the family I'd get tired of looking at books, but I never do. Anyway, I had an excuse: checking to see if they had my books in stock. Two of my cookbooks were there, and I found six paperback copies of *Murder in the Kitchen*. The hardcover had quickly gone out of print, but my publisher, Jake, had re-issued it in paperback the previous spring.

I wandered over to the historical section, and saw it right away: *The Romanovs: The Final Chapter* by Robert Massie, who'd written *Nicholas and Alexandra* years ago. Two minutes later, I had my MasterCard out again.

I flipped through the book while I ate at Say Cheese (cream of cauliflower soup, Caesar salad, mineral water, and a divine chocolate raspberry torte for dessert). Most of the book detailed the discovery and authentication of the Romanov bones in Ekaterinburg, Siberia, but a large part of the book was devoted to Anna Anderson. Massie re-told the story of her suicide attempt, internment in the mental hospital and her growing success as the Anastasia claimant. What was new was information about Franziska, who'd been found reading history books while everyone else in the village was bringing in the hay...

I took a taxi to Marlies Van Simp's house, which turned out to be in North London. A twenty-two dollar fare. I wasn't familiar with this part of the city, which seemed to have no part of the charm of the west end with its stately old houses or the liveliness of the east end. Fifteen years ago, this had probably all been farmland. Now, shopping malls and car dealerships mingled with newish subdivisions.

The Van Simp residence was an ordinary back-split with white aluminum siding and blue shutters. The garden, I noted, had been carefully prepared for winter, with bushes covered with burlap. A twine wreath hung on the blue front door. A Ford station wagon and a VW Jetta were parked in the driveway. I hoped the husband would not be there.

As I was paying the driver, the front door opened and Tetta Schwartz, followed by a younger, burly woman hurried out. Mrs. Schwartz looked over her shoulder and the other woman raised her fist at the slender, blonde woman who stood poised in the doorway. She did look like Marlene Dietrich, especially with that half-ironic, bemused smile on her face.

"Wait a sec," I asked the driver. He didn't turn the meter on again, and watched with me as the two women got into the Jetta. They were still talking angrily as the younger one crookedly backed the car out, bumping over the curb before she zipped away.

"Thanks. Sorry about that."

"Hey, that's okay. I see all kinds of stuff every day in this job."

I upped the tip by two dollars.

Close up, the resemblance to Marlene Dietrich was even more striking. It was the cool, distant poise more than anything, not only the way her blonde hair fell over one eye. She was a tall woman, and dressed in black silk pants and a classic white silk blouse, she looked fashionable in an ageless way. Her handshake, though, was limp.

She did not seem like a woman whose only son had recently been charged with murdering his father. I had expected someone softer, more vulnerable. Nor did she seem upset with what must have been a stormy session with her ex-mother-in-law. She's okay once you get to know her, Johnny had told me, I remembered with a pang. Poor Johnny. Not only had he had a dictator for a father, but his mother, on first impression anyway, appeared, in reality, to be a glamorous icicle.

She hung my coat up in an immaculate front closet. I glimpsed a mink coat. She wouldn't care what the animal rights people said. I placed my bag of books on the gleaming white tile floor.

"Come in, please, and sit down." Marlies Van Simp led me down three stairs to the sunken living room. Everything was white: white carpet, white sofa, white furniture, white drapes. The only colour came from a thick black coffee table with a turquoise and orange bowl on it and a yellowish landscape over a white library table with a white ceramic cat on it. The other picture, an abstract oil, was white and grey. I couldn't picture Johnny living in this house.

To my surprise, she opened a drawer on the end table and took out an ashtray and cigarettes. She offered me one, lit up and regarded me.

"I saw your mother-in-law leaving," I said.

"You have met her?" An eyebrow rose. She had the barest accent.

"Yes, she contacted me about your ex-husband and his Romanov interest."

"She is a witch. She thinks I have some of George's papers."

"She seemed pretty angry."

"I had to tell her to leave. Imagine, paying someone to drive her all this way. Her cleaning lady. She paid her cleaning lady to drive her."

"She wanted me to write about the Romanovs, just like your ex-husband did." I told her about meeting George years ago at Oktoberfest and seeing him again just before he was killed. It was hard to talk with those cool blue eyes watching and gauging me. I've talked to lots of people over the years in connection to the cookbooks and I usually find it easy to carry a conversation, but before long I was stammering, while she smoked and looked at me.

How did Johnny ever turn out to be such a personable, gentle young man with Marlies for a mother and George for a father? I wondered.

"So what did you think about the Anastasia story?" I asked. "I mean, Anna Anderson, I ah..." The Anastasia subject, ostensibly, was why I was seeing her.

"Oh, it was probably her. Anastasia. I think so. George believed it, and his mother also. But who is to know, for sure?"

"The DNA tests showed she was the Polish factory worker, Franziska."

"It would have been simple to make a mistake, no? A mistake on purpose. I think I believe she was Anastasia. Those are the papers my mother-in-law wanted, naturally."

"Oh?"

"But I did not hand them over. I am not a fool. To think I would hand them over, just like that! I know what those papers are worth. My husband and I have deposited them with our attorney who is trying to negotiate a sale. Of course we would be prepared to sell them to you for your book."

So that was why she had agreed to see me so readily.

"What kind of papers?"

"Letters, photographs. The material you would need for your book. It is all quite legal. George never paid me the money he owed me for the divorce settlement and so I retained the papers."

"How much are you asking?" It seemed wise to get right to the point.

"Fifty thousand," was the cool answer. "Our attorney is talking of auctioning the papers, but we would be prepared to sell them privately for that price."

"Sight unseen?"

"We can discuss that. I would be prepared to show you one or two items, naturally, but I would want to discuss this with our attorney. If you were to read them, what would be the benefit to another buyer? I'm sure there are many writers interested in such a book. But secrecy is of prime importance."

She lit another cigarette.

"Secrecy and the timing," she added.

"I'll have to think about this."

"But not too long, or we will find another buyer. By the way, my husband and I are impressed with your credentials. We looked you up in the library."

"The London library does have most of my books."

"You would make a lot of money with this book. The papers would be a good investment for you."

"I guess the fifty thousand would be useful for Johnny's legal fees," I said. "You really think he killed his father?"

For a moment, her face shifted. But it was anger I saw there, not sorrow. "George was difficult," she said. "A hard man to live with. But even so, I cannot believe my son killed his father. My husband, on the other hand, believes Johnny killed George. It is a difficult situation."

"I can understand that. It must be hard for you. Johnny's lawyer thinks someone connected to the Romanovs killed your ex-husband. Someone who knew I was coming to interview him about Anastasia and who wanted to prevent him from telling me what he knew."

"That is possible. I entirely believe this possibility. George always said it was about the money. The Tsar had millions and naturally everyone wanted them. Perhaps only Anna Anderson knew where it was, and she would not tell until she was recognized."

"You're saying that Anna Anderson told George..."

"Anything is possible. Shall we have coffee?"

I accepted. Where did she think I would get fifty thousand

dollars? I wondered. Like many people, she assumed all writers made mega bucks. Even though Anna Anderson wasn't Anastasia, I wished I could see the papers. As Mark believed, Anna Anderson/Franziska could have been given information by people who really had secret information.

I was glad Marion wasn't with me. She'd be wracking her brains now, trying to think of ways she could mortgage the house so she could come up with fifty thousand dollars...

Could Mark somehow get those papers, subpoena them— subpoena Marlies— if the papers related to his case?

Marlies returned with a wooden tray holding two thin red coffee cups, a jug of heated milk and a little bowl of cubed sugar, just like her ex-husband had served with his coffee.

At least the coffee gave me some time to try to get the conversation onto a more personal level, but as hard as I tried to mention Johnny casually, saying I had met him a few times and liked him, the harder, and less casually, did she steer the conversation back to the papers. She admitted that it hadn't been easy raising a son on her own and that, yes, her husband had not always gotten along with Johnny, but soon she was repeating how valuable the papers were, and how they would surely sell for more than fifty thousand on "the open market." She hinted that she had letters written by Anna Anderson and that the information contained in these letters was shattering.

"But if this information would help Johnny's case, maybe you should think of letting Mark see them."

"But you see, the letters have nothing to do with what has happened. They would not point to anyone. I can assure you I would hand the papers over if for one moment I felt they would help my son."

"Why don't you let Mark be the judge of that?"

"We are following the advice of our attorney."

After an hour, there was not much more to say. I asked her to call me a taxi. To my surprise, she offered to drive me to the train station. I said the train did not leave until 5:30, and that I'd poke around downtown in the meantime. Fine; she'd drive me downtown.

Marlies seemed to be one of those people it was impossible to stand up to, and I was still protesting when she pulled on a trench coat and beige driving gloves. She would drive me; there was absolutely no need to take a taxi, she said.

She was an aggressive driver, talking and not paying attention to the road, as if what she had to say was the most important thing in the world. I would not be disappointed in the papers, she said, and I need have no fear that the papers were not legally hers. The papers would make my book; there was no question about that. She wanted me to have the papers, not someone she had not met or could not trust. She could trust me, she felt.

By the time we arrived at La Galleria, I hadn't said two words.

"Let us set a date then," she said, drawing to the curb at the mall. She paid no attention to the driver behind her who tooted his horn. "Shall we say a week?"

"I'll have to discuss this with my husband."

"But naturally. It is an important decision, but I can assure you that you will not regret it."

"It's a great deal of money," I said weakly.

"You will come out ahead; far, far ahead." She extended her hand; we shook. I escaped, clutching my books.

The trouble with carrying books is that they are heavy, but their burden didn't trouble me as I wandered around the mall. I had several hours to kill, and I spent it wandering through the household department at The Bay, trying on a dress at Laura Ashley's, and sampling the perfume at Eaton's. A few of the stores had Christmas decorations up. I bought coffee mugs with roosters on them and placemats to match, as well as a pair of Birkenstocks reduced to

$39.99. As I presented my MasterCard for the last purchase, I realized I'd spent well over a hundred bucks that day, but it was far short of the fifty thousand I could never shell out.

Chapter Eleven

"You should look at Marlies as the murderer. If anyone could be a cold-blooded killer, she's it," I told Mark the next night.

I'd invited Mark and Emma for dinner. And Thomas, in whose honour I served chili in a pumpkin shell, which he said was neat. With wild rice and cornbread, it wasn't one of my more exotic menus, but Mark hadn't been sure what time he could get away. Emma and Thomas (and Kelly) drove in from the country, but Mark didn't get there until seven. By then, a starving Thomas had already eaten supper. Now he was ensconced on the couch, with a dog on each side, a big bowl of popcorn on his lap, and a video on the TV.

"Unfortunately the dragon lady has an alibi. She and husband number two spent the night in Windsor." Mark lifted his Molson Dry and took a swig. "They stayed at the Holiday Inn."

"They could have rented a room, raced to the nursery, stolen the papers and shot George. Presumably Hans knew her. Then they could have hidden the gun in Johnny's van. She might easily have known where Johnny spent the night," I said.

"Sorry. They had dinner with her husband's brother," Mark said.

"And she wouldn't have pinned it on her son," Emma protested. "Even if she is the Dragon Lady, she wouldn't want her son charged with murder."

"Pretty cool customer," Mark said. "When it comes to saving their own hides, people will do anything. Women have killed their kids. Everyone says men are the violent ones, but how about these women who do away with their kids?"

"In a moment of anger, maybe," Emma conceded. "If a woman's poor and has no money, no support, and maybe she's drinking and the kids are driving her insane... I can understand that, I can see how it could happen."

"Marlies isn't saying Johnny did it, but she won't hand over the papers."

"She wasn't going to bail him out at first," Mark said. "But she'd have looked like a total shit if she didn't."

Emma shook her head and reached for the wine bottle. Her face was flushed.

"There may be a legal way to get the papers," Mark said. "She could be withholding evidence."

"She even admits someone connected to the Romanovs could have killed her ex," I said.

Mark drummed his fingers on the table.

"You have to find who planted the gun," I said. "That's what you have to do. Find the person who planted the gun and Johnny's off the hook."

"Right," Mark agreed, as Thomas wandered in with the empty popcorn bowl. I stuck another package of popcorn into the micro-wave. Conrad and Kelly panted at Thomas' side. Both dogs were pigs, he said. They'd eaten most of the popcorn.

"I gather you no longer think Johnny's guilty," Mark said. "Maybe you're coming around to my way of thinking."

"I don't know. The Romanov thing is just so bizarre..."

"You're not kidding," Peter said.

I ignored him.

"What if Marlies sells the papers to someone else?" I asked Mark.

"She won't sell the papers," Mark said, "because I'm going to advise her she'll be subpoenaed and that her icy cold neck will be on the block if she attempts to destroy evidence. I wouldn't mind seeing those papers. George and his mother both talked about the money. Anna Anderson had been told about the money by people who didn't want the legitimate Romanov heirs to get their hands on the fortune. What you have to ask yourself is who are these people? And why did they want to keep the money out of the hands of the Romanovs?"

"To keep it themselves," I suggested. "Anna Anderson would be acknowledged, receive the money, and share it with her supporters."

"But she wouldn't be acknowledged because she wasn't Anastasia, she was Franziska, and I think her enemies would have proved that conclusively if the court ruled in her favour by presenting the real Anastasia."

"Who was living in Guelph," Peter quipped.

Mark didn't pay any attention to this. "This of course brings us to a quandary, because the natural question is, why not produce the real Anastasia, or the one sister who survived? She would naturally get the money. But it's not so simple. Perhaps, if the real Anastasia survived, she did not want the Soviets to know. In any case, the court fights with Anna Anderson put any money on hold. I've read there was no money left in western banks but I find that hard to believe. I think Anna Anderson's supporters were somehow directed, manipulated, by people who did not want the Romanovs to have any power. By people who wanted to divide the family."

The doorbell rang, and Conrad and Kelly went crazy. Peter held the barking dogs back so I could answer the door. Peter was so surprised he let the dogs go, but our visitor wasn't bothered by the dogs' jumping.

"Guess what? I'm moving to Guelph!"

Peter's sister, Allison, dumped two plastic suitcases into the hall and held the door open for her three boys.

Chapter Twelve

We put Allison and six-year-old Timmy in the spare room. Matthew and Jody bedded down in sleeping bags on the living room floor.

She had quit the job at Roan's Drugstore the same day she started because Joe drove by with this woman, Belinda, in the truck. "I hung up my smock and walked right out of there," was how Allison put it. And that night she stole Joe's truck ("If he thinks another woman is riding in that truck, he has another think coming!"), loaded it with kids and suitcases and garbage bags stuffed with clothes, and drove to Guelph.

Allison's plans were that she would work in The Bookworm and I would care for the kids after school. When she was settled she'd look for an apartment.

"I mean, it's the perfect solution," she said at breakfast. "Why should I work up north in that two-horse town when my own brother has a business I can work in? And since you don't have a job or anything. you can watch the kids for an hour or two after school."

She lit a cigarette. The boys, tired after their long drive, were still asleep, but Allison was perky. With her reddish hair pulled back in a pony tail and the freckles on her pale skin, she looked about eighteen.

"She's family, what can you do?" I'd said to Peter the night before when finally, at three, we crawled into bed. We hadn't been able to get to the dishes until one-thirty. First we had to get the boys settled, and then Allison had to fill us in on the terrible times she'd been through. Her marriage was finis, kaput, and then Hugh was angry because she went drinking at the Meredith Hotel ("The old fogey just doesn't understand that I have to have some fun!"). And she couldn't count on Marion to babysit because she was always off in that car of hers, with no consideration for anyone but herself!

"You're going to miss Meredith," I said. "You've never lived anywhere else."

"Time I did. That hick town. Honestly, Carolyn, it's nothing but a dump. Mom and Dad were always after me to get out, go to university, but I went and married Joe instead. What a fool I was. Maybe I'll take some university courses in the fall. I'll juggle the hours I work."

"The problem is, Peter already has two people working for him."

"He'll just have to let one of them go or something." She shrugged, unconcerned. Peter would only be too glad to get rid of Muriel, but I doubted if he'd hire Allison. As far as Peter was concerned, Allison could head back up north again, but I knew if it came right down to it, he'd help her get established in Guelph. Families. Growing up as an only child in my grandmother's home, I'd never experienced the love-hate sibling relationship Allison and Peter shared, but I knew Peter wouldn't show Allison and her kids the door.

"What about breakfast? What do the boys usually eat?"

"What kind of cereal do you have?"

"Corn flakes, some porridge."

"They like that junk with sugar on it. But they can have corn flakes today. They'll eat it if they're hungry enough."

"That's okay. I'll run out and get them what they like."

"To hell with it. Let them eat corn flakes."

"I don't mind." Allison didn't argue, but asked me to pick her up two "packs of smokes." She handed over a twenty, the last of her money, she said.

I loaded Conrad in the car and headed over to the A&P. It went through my head that I could run away. I could see Allison living with us for years, cluttering up the house with the boys and their belongings, with the sleeping bags and t-shirts and sneakers. It wasn't that I didn't like her kids— I did— but to have all of them living with us, in a small house, was another matter.

And her assumption that I would automatically be free to look after the kids because I didn't have a "job or anything" infuriated me. I wasn't close to Allison; I didn't have anything in common with her. To tell the truth, I didn't really like the woman. I could see how Marion felt.

At the grocery store, I phoned Marion from a pay phone, but no one was home. Did they realize where Allison was? I wondered. There was the matter of the truck, too. Joe would be furious, and for all I knew he was on his way down to Guelph to retrieve his precious vehicle.

For now, there was nothing to do but to buy groceries, and I filled the cart with three kinds of sugary cereal, frozen pizza and waffles, Kraft dinner, popcorn, canned soup— all the kinds of stuff Allison always had in her kitchen cupboards. Overdone roast was her usual company repertoire, and the meat was often venison.

Soda pop? Why not? The kids swilled it in Meredith. But extra milk, too, and orange juice. Packaged cookies. Oreos and chocolate chip.

My cart was heaped high by the time I wheeled it to the cash. At the next lane, a chubby two-year-old girl ate chips while her mother unloaded junk food similar to mine. The woman tried to put the opened bag of chips on the conveyor belt, but the child squawked. "Give me that or it'll go right into the garbage!" More yells.

The mother's eyes met mine, then went to my purchases.

"Yours must all be in school," she remarked. "Aren't you lucky!"

On the way out of the store, I stopped and bought Allison her cigarettes.

The TV was blaring when I returned and the house was filled with cigarette smoke. Allison was on the telephone. The boys were still in their pyjamas and no one had tidied up the sleeping bags. Empty cereal dishes sat on the coffee table.

"Hiya kids, I see you had breakfast."

"Corn flakes, we had corn flakes 'cause there wasn't nothing else," Timmy said cheerfully as I gathered up the plates before Conrad could lick the dregs. Conrad was too fast for me, though, and his nose landed in a dish, spilling the milk. He lapped it off the floor while Timmy laughed. Matthew took the other two plates from me and headed to the kitchen, leaving Jody with his eyes glued to the set, where a high-speed chase was taking place in what looked like San Francisco.

"Does your mother let you watch stuff like that?" I asked, perching on the edge of the couch. Timmy crawled on my lap.

"We can watch anything we want," Jody said.

"But Gram doesn't let us watch everything," Timmy said. "Not guns and stuff.

"Or kissing," he added with a grin, as shots rang out on the screen.

Should I get the kids to at least roll the sleeping bags up? I wondered. The idea was tempting but maybe I was being too rigid. In any case, I didn't have to suggest any such thing, because Matthew returned and began tidying up. Matthew was the one who'd spent the most time with Marion. She'd even taught him to knit, although Joe had put a stop to that in short order.

"Come help me unpack the groceries," I told Timmy. "There just might be some goodies in there for you guys."

Allison was lighting one cigarette off another.

"That was Joe, Mr. Asshole himself," she said. "He says if I don't get the truck back he'll call the cops on me."

"I told you you shouldn't have taken the truck," Matthew said from the doorway. He had the sleeping bags folded over his arms.

"Never you mind! It's not your worry."

Matthew shrugged and asked what he should do with the sleeping bags. I told him to stow them in the spare room.

"But I know what the cops'll tell him. They'll say I have every right to his old truck, since I'm his wife. If he wants it he can just come down and get the old thing. I can get around without it very well. It's a good thing I know how to drive a standard."

Our car was a standard.

"Well, if I'm not using my car, but I..."

"I thought I'd run out this afternoon and pick up a few outfits. Did you remember my smokes?"

She eyed Timmy, rummaging in the bags of groceries. I took the cigarettes out of my purse and handed them to her, plus the change from the twenty.

"That's not a lot for clothes," I said.

"I'll use plastic. Anyway, the child support comes due the end of the month. I guess I better pick up some skirts or something for the store."

I wasn't going to argue with her about The Bookworm. Peter could tell her she wasn't going to work for him, I thought.

"I could drop you off at a mall," I offered. "I've got to do some research this afternoon."

"Research? I thought I'd get you to keep the kids while I look around."

"Sorry, Allison. It has to be today." I might as well start putting my foot down right away, I thought. "I really do have things to do."

"You don't have a boss or job or anything!"

"But I have commitments."

"I can't go shopping with the boys. Matthew especially. He hates malls. And what if Joe turns up for the truck and no one's home?"

"He'll just have to come back. Or wait."

"This is great, just great," Allison muttered.

I didn't answer and busied myself putting groceries away. The Sugar Pops had a favour in them and I gave Timmy a bowl so he could dump the cereal out. Matthew came back and handed me cans to put away in the cupboards.

"What about that friend of yours from last night?" Allison asked. "Could she keep the kids?"

"Emma? I'd hate to ask her. Thomas is in school all day and she's busy with her quilts. I wouldn't want to ask her unless it's a real emergency."

"This is an emergency," Allison said.

I didn't respond to this.

"So how about it, Matthew? You want to come with me?" I asked him. Sure, he said.

"How do you know this Emma won't keep my kids if you don't ask?" Allison wanted to know.

"I just wouldn't feel right asking her."

"Joe always said people were unfriendly down south," Allison said. She lit another cigarette. Matthew opened a window.

"If we're staying here aren't you supposed to register us for school?" Matthew asked Allison. "You can buy clothes when we're in school."

"Don't be smart."

Matthew sighed.

"So is Joe coming down for the truck or what?" I wanted to know. "He wouldn't get here until late this afternoon anyway. You know he won't call the police."

Allison shrugged.

"Who's going to drive him?"

"I bet his mother," Allison said. "He wouldn't dare bring that slut Belinda down here. He says he just gave her a lift, but I know better."

"Dad needs the truck for work," Matthew said. "We should have come down by bus or something."

"Or something. Yeah."

"Maybe Gram will drive him," Matthew said. "So are we going to school here or not?"

"No, I'm putting you all to work in a factory!"

"Let's have some lunch," I said. "Who's for pizza?"

The "research," of course, had been a lie, and inviting Matthew along complicated things because I now had to do something. I decided to visit Johnny again, and after I dropped Allison and the other kids off at the mall, I filled Matthew in on the bare bones of the story. He knew all about Anastasia because Marion had talked to him about it. He'd even read *Nicholas and Alexandra*! Matthew did well in school, and Marion had always encouraged him to read.

"Gram says I'm just like Uncle Peter," Matthew said. He blushed. I resisted the impulse to ruffle his hair. He didn't look like Peter, being heavier and darker, but for a moment he sounded just like his uncle. Serious, a little abashed. A bit nerdy? But I didn't think the kids in Meredith teased him the way they had Peter, who'd been the original nerd right through school.

"So what do you think of this Anastasia story?"

"I don't think Anna Anderson was Anastasia. But it's a mystery and people like mysteries, like about the princes in the tower and like that. Like Joan of Arc not really dying."

"I don't know that story."

"People said someone else was burned instead. Witnesses said the real Joan of Arc lived on and got married."

"Well, this is a real life mystery. Who killed Johnny's father? You can watch and listen and tell me what you think later on. You can help me with more research, too."

"If we're here that long. I bet Mom'll go right back to Meredith. That's why she didn't put us in school right away."

"Do you want to go back to Meredith?"

He shrugged. Meredith could be limiting, he said. Those were his exact words, probably copied from Marion.

"Mom just wants Dad to come chasing after her and say he's sorry. They always fight. I guess I'm used to it."

He sounded resigned.

"I know what," I told him. "Whatever happens, I want you to choose a whole stack of books at The Bookworm. How does that sound? We'll stop at the store on our way home."

"Does Peter have Sci Fi? Because when I'm not reading history I'm kind of into Sci Fi."

"Tons of Sci Fi."

"But Peter has to pay for the books, doesn't he?"

"Not the price the public pays. But that's okay. Really. I love buying books for people, especially for nephews who help me with research!"

A purple van painted with psychedelic flowers was parked at the Old Hanover Nursery.

"Johnny must have friends visiting. Some of his friends are musicians," I told Matthew.

"Maybe we should come back another time," Matthew said.

"Of course we shouldn't come back another time. The more we find out the better."

"If I'd known what was up, I would have brought my tape recorder. It's just small. I could have hidden it under my shirt."

"You'll just have to use your excellent brain instead. Your powers of recall."

"How will you explain being here?"

"I'll just say we were in the neighbourhood."

"What about Conrad?" Conrad was already barking.

"We'll leave him in the car. I don't see Hans anywhere about."

"Hans, the German Shepherd who was guarding the body?"

"See, you don't need a tape recorder. Your memory's excellent. I only mentioned Hans once."

"Grampa says I should become a policeman like him."

"Do you want to?"

"Nah, Dad says cops are crooks." Matthew followed this statement quickly with, "Of course, Grampa's not a crook."

If Johnny was surprised to see us, he didn't show it. His friend's name was Plymouth Orlando and he had a long grey beard, although the rest of his hair was orange. Plymouth wasn't just skinny, he was skeletal. He wore an embroidered scarlet shirt that came almost to his knees and Johnny and Plymouth were drinking herbal tea. Lemon chamomile, to be exact.

Plymouth played the harp. "My friend Plymouth, the harpist," is how Johnny introduced him.

"I don't think I've ever met a harpist before," I said.

"I used to play the drums," Plymouth said, "but the harp is more peaceful."

His voice was soft and gentle. Despite his rather weird appearance, his eyes were intelligent and kind. I saw Matthew blink. He would never have met anyone like Plymouth in Meredith.

"Plymouth's less violent than the rest of us," Johnny said. He poured tea for Matthew and me.

"I wouldn't call you violent," Plymouth said quietly to Johnny.

"I'm speaking relatively. You've heard the saying, 'He wouldn't hurt a fly?' Well, Plymouth really wouldn't. He doesn't even kill mosquitoes."

Plymouth laughed, not at all insulted.

"Speaking of other-than-human species, where's Hans?"

"Asleep on my bed. He went nuts when Plymouth arrived, but Plymouth gave him a massage and Hans is now in some kind of dream state."

"Well, maybe you could massage my dog," I said. "My little monster, Conrad."

We talked about dogs for a while. And cats. Plymouth had three cats, Snoopy, Lear, and Mozart. Snoopy was the oldest, almost twenty, and named before, as Plymouth said, "I went into the artistic mode. In other words, I was a kid and didn't know any better."

"He even played hockey," Johnny said. "And shot little rabbits."

"You did?" Matthew asked incredulously.

I explained that Matthew was from Meredith, where real men went hunting. Plymouth nodded; he'd grown up in a town that sounded like Meredith, he said.

"My father goes hunting," Matthew said. "And he kills mosquitoes, too!" he blurted. "Do you think mosquitoes are reincarnated people? Is that why you don't kill them?"

"I guess I just don't like killing things any more," Plymouth said.

"So how do you keep from getting bit? You use a spray or what?"

"I take Vitamin B. The mosquitoes don't seem to like the smell on your body. But I don't get bitten very often. Insects seem to realize I mean them no harm."

Matthew shook his head.

"I bet you're a vegetarian," I said.

"Have been for years, but I try not to make a big deal of it. In other words if someone invites me for dinner, I try and eat around the meat."

"I'm a vegetarian, too," Johnny said. "At least now I am. Dad used to cook meat. German food, schnitzel and pork. Sometimes I'd eat it, just to keep the peace. Not eating meat was just another crazy thing I did, in his books. He always said if I'd gone through the post-war period in Germany when there was nothing, I wouldn't be so fussy."

Plymouth looked at him. I thought Plymouth would not mention the murder because Matthew was there, and I was right, because Plymouth began asking questions about Conrad. He didn't have much time today, he said, but he'd be glad to give Conrad a full massage another time.

As a matter of fact he should be on his way, he said. He wanted to be back in Guelph for three, which was when he did his afternoon meditation.

"At least meet my dog," I said, and we all trooped outside so Plymouth could look at Conrad.

Who snarled at Plymouth, baring his teeth.

"I don't think he's ever seen anyone with a beard before," I said.

"Well, I do look pretty strange," Plymouth said. "I do admit to that."

Plymouth opened the car door.

"I don't think— " I put out a restraining hand, ready to grab Conrad by the scruff of the neck, but Plymouth, totally unafraid and speaking in a soft, muted voice, stretched out his hand to Conrad.

Conrad lunged. Plymouth pulled his hand back just in time.

"No, bad dog! Bad!" I grabbed Conrad and rolled him over on his back and sat on him. "Bad boy, bad boy! No biting!"

Plymouth looked at Conrad sadly. He started to bend down, but I waved him back.

"I don't know what's gotten into him. I've never seen him like this before," I said from my crouching position. Conrad was still growling deep in his throat. "It has to be your beard," I explained, embarrassed.

Plymouth actually had tears in his eyes as he got into his flowered van and drove away.

I released Conrad as soon as Plymouth was gone. Conrad gave a final growl, but when Johnny said, "Here boy, here," he came bounding over to Johnny and licked his face.

"I think your dog has given poor Plymouth a nervous breakdown," Johnny said. Conrad circled around him, wanting to play. "He'll never get over this. He even approached a wild moose once and petted it."

"Maybe the moose was used to men with beards."

Johnny shook his head and threw a stick for Conrad.

"Is Plymouth a good friend of yours?" I asked.

"Pretty good. He looks weird but he's a really neat guy. One of the kindest people I've ever met. He's been out here a few times since Dad died. My father, as you can imagine, hated him. Made fun of him. Fairy, you know."

"Gay?"

"Pretty radical, actually. But that doesn't matter to me. Beneath that rather flamboyant exterior he's got a lot of common sense."

Matthew was all ears.

"I liked Plymouth," I said.

"Of course, that's not his real name. You could say he's re-invented himself. He used to work in a bank, but I didn't know him then. Now he cleans offices to make a few bucks, and plays his harp when he gets a chance. He shares this house in Guelph with some other people. It's where I stay sometimes. Not all of them are gay."

"That doesn't matter."

"I'm thinking of asking Plymouth to help me at the nursery here. If everything works out, court and all. Plymouth, as you can imagine, has a real green thumb."

"I'm sure he does." But would he drive customers away, the suburbanites who came to buy shrubs and planting sets? I thought suddenly of Mabel and could just imagine what she'd have to say about this addition to the neighbourhood. "I should probably get going, too. I have to pick Matthew's mother and his brothers up in town. They're all down from Meredith."

"Visiting?"

"Not sure. They might stay."

"We might be going to school here," Matthew interjected.

"I want to invite you for dinner one night," I told Johnny.

"Sure. Love to come."

"Don't worry, no meat."

"I'm not like Plymouth. He mainly eats lentils and grains. That's why he's so thin."

"Friday? Sevenish?"

"Sure. Great."

"Tell me one thing. Does Plymouth know all about the Anastasia story?"

"You bet. He thinks Anna Anderson was a disturbed, pitiful soul. He's quite interested in the story. He would have liked to discuss her with my father, but of course that wasn't in the cards."

"And what does he think happened to your father?"

Johnny said, "Plymouth thinks it happened because of the Anastasia story and what my father knew, or thought he knew. He thinks I was set up."

"I'd like to invite Plymouth for dinner, too. Is that okay? Do you think he'll come? After what happened with Conrad?"

"I think he'd love to come. To redeem himself with Conrad."

"Should I invite him, or could you?"

"I can. Or you can ask him yourself. I'll get you the address."

"Don't they have a phone?"

"Sometimes they don't answer it. If Plymouth is home and meditating, or reading, he simply unplugs the phone. Actually, I don't think I've ever talked to Plymouth on the telephone."

"I've never met anyone who's gay before," Matthew said as we drove to The Bookworm. "I mean, we learn about AIDS and stuff at school, but I don't think there are any gay people in Meredith."

"I'm sure there are some. But in a small town people tend to conform. Plymouth came from a small town, and he probably didn't tell anyone there he was gay."

"He was really nice once you forgot how he dressed."

"I think he feels his dress is a form of self-expression."

Matthew shook his head.

"He's not hurting anyone. He's clean. Why shouldn't he dress the way he wants to dress?"

"He just looked so strange. People would sure stare at him in Meredith."

"Some people stare at him in Guelph, I'm sure. But so what?"

"And Conrad hated him!"

"I think Conrad was spooked by the beard. He was probably asleep in the car and woke up to see this face with hair all over it."

"You'll have to lock Conrad in the bedroom or basement if Plymouth comes for dinner. And what's Mom gonna say about Plymouth?"

"What should she say? He's my guest. I'm sure she'll be polite."

"And how will we all fit around the table?"

"I can add leaves to the table." Or the younger kids could eat earlier, I thought.

If they were still there, and not back in Meredith.

"Never mind worrying about dinner, Matthew. What about your impressions? What do you think?"

"I think Johnny could never in a million years hurt anybody," Matthew said fervently. "Maybe someone in Plymouth's house planted the gun. Is that why you're going there?"

"The thought did occur to me."

"Maybe I can come with you."

"If you're not in school by then."

"I bet Mom'll keep us out because she's really going back to Meredith."

At The Bookworm, I found a flustered Muriel looking after Jody and Timmy. She had them sitting down with markers in their hands, but Timmy's face was tear-stained and he ran to me as soon as he saw me. Muriel shook her head and motioned for me to come to the back room.

"It was terrible," she said, after I handed a comforted Timmy over to Matthew. "I have never seen anything like it. The mother and children arrived in a taxi. She practically dragged the youngest one in by the arm, the poor little thing. And I hear they're all moving to Guelph." She shook her head. "And you saddled with them, too."

"Where are they now? Peter and his sister?"

"Peter took her for coffee," Muriel said with disapproval.

"What was the trouble?"

"Oh, the little fellow kept crying he missed his Daddy. Poor tyke. He wants to go home and see Daddy and Gram, he said. I sat him down with the markers and he drew a picture of his cat, but then he cried that he missed his cat. It's always the children who suffer when a family breaks up."

But then Muriel changed gears.

"Your husband and his sister don't get along very well, do they? I've seen it happen before. My husband didn't get along with his sister, and until the day he died they only exchanged words at Christmas. His sister's certainly different from Peter."

"Yes, they're not much alike."

Matthew, holding Timmy by the hand, came to the back. Timmy had to go to the bathroom.

I wandered out to the front, where Jody, looking too big at nine for the kiddy table and the markers, stared into space. He didn't notice me. A single tear ran down his cheek.

I thought suddenly of arriving at my grandmother's house in Maine and watching my mother drive away. An old memory. I was five years old. It wasn't something I thought about too often, but I knew that for a long time, every night when I went to bed I prayed to God that He would bring my alcoholic, man-crazy mother back. He never did.

These little kids were people, with feelings, and I felt small and mean for having resented their presence in our home.

It was a deflated Allison who arrived back at the store with Peter ten minutes later. Peter shook his head at me as she tucked Timmy's shirt into his jeans and wiped his nose, while Muriel stood by with a nosy, tut-tut look on her face. Without a word to anyone, Allison herded her children out of the store. Matthew looked back at me: I'd forgotten his books.

"She looks like her heart is breaking," I said, following Allison. Peter's hand fell on my shoulder. He waited until we were outside the store to tell me that he'd informed Allison that there was no job for her at The Bookworm.

"So now what?"

Peter sighed and shook his head. "She's determined not to go back to Meredith. She'll have to find something else. It's not that I'm not tempted to let Muriel ago, but it just wouldn't work with Allison in the store. She's got to find an apartment, too. I'd like to boot her out, but we can't."

"It's all right. I know."

"It's going to be a circus."

Allison was getting back out of the car, and Conrad was right behind her. Without a word to Peter she returned to the store. The kids scrambled out after Conrad, who jumped up on Peter.

"A circus," Peter said to me. "What's your mother doing?" he asked the kids.

Allison had forgotten her shopping. She emerged from The Bookworm carrying a large Reitman's bag. Matthew seized Conrad's collar and dragged him to the car. Allison was lighting a cigarette.

At home, the truck was gone. A note in the mailbox informed Allison that Joe had picked the truck up, using the second set of keys. Would she kindly mail her set to him?

Without a word, Allison went to her bedroom. I cooked spaghetti and meat balls for the kids.

After dinner, I went to our bedroom and called Marion. I hadn't talked to her since she left, and we both pretended there hadn't been any friction between us.

The first topic to be discussed was, of course, Allison.

"She should not be imposing on you. She has never been the most considerate human being, I'm afraid," Marion sighed. "You're not used to the kids and the commotion."

"I suppose she wanted to put some distance between herself and Joe. She really had nowhere else to go, I guess. If she stays in Guelph, we'll help her to find an apartment."

"You'll have to push her out, I'm afraid. She'll want you to babysit. You have to be firm with Allison. You go about your business, do what you have to do. How is Peter taking it?"

"He told her she couldn't work at The Bookworm."

"I expected she'd want to work there when I heard she'd gone to Guelph."

"You mean you didn't know?"

"Joe told us. Dear me."

"He picked up the truck while Allison was out. I think she's disappointed he didn't stick around. I must say I'm surprised, too. I thought Joe would be weeping and wailing to get Allison back to Meredith."

"I, however, am not surprised. His mother drove to Guelph and I am sure she told him not to wait. How did Allison take it?"

"Badly. She went to her room. Do you want to speak to her?"

"Let her calm down first. We had a little disagreement a few days before she left. She wanted my car to go shopping in North Bay and I said no."

"Oh."

"Yes, it's probably my fault that she's landed on your doorstep. But I had an appointment to drive to Barrie to speak to an old man whose brother had been Tsar Nicholas' guard."

"No!"

"Oh, yes. In Ekaterinburg, where the Romanovs were shot. The brother was adamant that one of the girls got away. Some historians claimed there were posters saying Anastasia was missing, and apparently the brother had seen one. Of course the brother was evacuated to Perm before the Whites arrived in Ekaterinburg, but he definitely said one of the girls was missing!

"The brother believed Anna Anderson could have been Anastasia, but I've just read something else in a British paper. A woman claiming to be Anastasia was alive in Russia until the nineteen-seventies! They kept her in a mental hospital, but the only unusual thing about her was her claim to be Anastasia. Apparently she wrote letters in schoolgirl German and French to her uncle, George V. There was a picture of her."

"And?"

"An elderly woman, but she looked like the Romanovs to me."

"Anna Anderson must always have been afraid the real Anastasia would emerge one day. If she knew so much about the Russian royal family, she must have known about the real Anastasia."

"Unless she believed she really was Anastasia. You know, I'm afraid I'm losing faith in Anna Anderson. The books I have been reading! In one, this Baron von Kleist, who first took her out of the mental hospital in Berlin in 1922, caught her copying a telephone number out of the directory and she ate the paper! But then, here's something else, a few years later. The Duke of Leuchtenberg put her

up at his castle in Bavaria. When she arrived, he showed her her suite
and the view of the little lake and she dismissed him with a curt 'Good
night'! Would a girl from a peasant family have acted this way with
a Duke living in a castle? I ask you that?"

"She acted like royalty."

"Like haughty, selfish royalty. She acted like Anastasia's mother,
Empress Alexandra, actually. The Empress and Anna Anderson both
got red blotches on their skin when they were upset and angry."

"But if Anna Anderson was emotionally disturbed..."

"Oh, she was, she was. She spent over a year in a private clinic
in the States at the end of the twenties, if you'll recall. One of the
doctors who examined her in Germany said she had this inner
haughtiness, this pathological attitude..."

"And this same attitude would convince people she was royal."

"Yes."

"Unless she really did believe she was Anastasia."

"But it comes to the same thing in the end, doesn't it? Mad or
sane, people believed her."

We chatted another half an hour about Anastasia. Marion's talk
about castles and old titles and ladies-in-waiting made me forget about
the blaring TV in the living room (Peter had gone out for videos)
where Peter, I imagined, had fallen into a bored sleep among his
nephews.

I wished Marion could visit (our semi-quarrel was forgotten),
and I said so, but of course space was limited with Allison and the
kids at our place. Perhaps she could stay at Emma's? I suggested, but
Marion wouldn't hear of it.

"Tell the kids I'll call them tomorrow night at seven."

"That's fine. Peter and I will be taking Conrad to school, but
they'll be here. Unless they want to come along..."

"Never mind. You and Peter get out alone. Tell them they have
to stay at home for my call."

"So what should I do?" Allison asked me the next morning. Breakfast was over, and she'd sent the kids outside. ("Go play on the street or something.") Cereal bowls and half-empty milk glasses covered the table and already the ashtray was overflowing.

"If you're going to stay, I suppose you should enrol the kids in school. That would be the first thing, I guess."

"But should I stay? It would have been different if I could have worked for Peter. I'm pretty upset about that, by the way. He could have hired me. I know he doesn't care for that old biddy he has working for him."

"But he can't just fire her. And anyway, maybe it's not the best place to work, for family."

"But it would have been something. I don't know where to start."

"Read the want ads. Try the unemployment office."

"No one's hiring these days, with the economy the way it is. I don't know. I just assumed I'd be working for Peter. He probably expects me to waitress or something. I didn't come down here to sell hamburgers and beer."

"You could get on your feet that way, though."

"Joe's supposed to send me money at the end of the month. If he tries to weasel out of that I'll kill him."

"You could have it deducted from his pay. I think that's what they do now."

"What pay? He's self-employed. He'll just say he's not making anything. I bet his mother drove him down to get the truck."

I hadn't told her about talking to Marion, but Allison saw from my face that she was right.

"She's only too glad I'm out of there, the old bitch. I'm glad I wasn't here when they came for the truck! But the nerve of him— leaving me without a vehicle! You're not using your car today, are you?"

"Later on…"

"How can I register the boys at school without a car? And look for a job?"

"I'll drive you to the school. And to the unemployment office. But I'll need my car later on." I did want to go to Plymouth's house to invite him to dinner Friday night.

"And how am I supposed to get to a job if I find one? What if I'm a waitress, working nights?"

"Look, Allison, no one's pushing you to do anything. You can stay here until you get on your feet. You can take your time looking for a job. You don't have to push the panic button. You and your kids have a place to live. Nothing's settled yet. You might even go back to Meredith."

"Never." But she sounded doubtful.

No, Allison said after a tomato soup and egg salad sandwich lunch, she wasn't registering her kids for school today. She'd have to do a wash first; she'd left Meredith with a bunch of dirty laundry.

"You go off and do your thing. I'll do the laundry. Maybe I'll call Unemployment."

"I'll bring a Guelph newspaper home."

"You wouldn't want to take the kids along, I guess."

"Well, Matthew— "

"You can't take just one. Favouring one over the others. And Matthew keeps Jody and Timmy out of my hair. Without him here, I'll go nuts in my present state of mind."

I agreed to take all the kids. But she would have to look after Conrad.

I still had not fulfilled my promise to Matthew to buy him the books.

"Now, I have to visit some people," I told the boys in the car, "and I hope it won't take too long. Afterwards we'll go to the mall, okay? And then to The Bookworm for Matthew. How does that sound?"

Bribery, bribery. Be good or you won't get anything.

"I want a rabbit," Timmy said. "Can we go to a pet store so I can get a rabbit?"

"You're not supposed to ask," Jody pointed out. "Anyway, Mom already said you couldn't have a rabbit because they chew the furniture."

"They have to chew or their teeth get too big," Matthew explained.

"I'd keep it in a pen," Timmy said. "You get a pen with a rabbit and a leash so you can take it for walks."

"Rabbits don't walk. They hop, silly nut," Jody said.

"I'm not a silly nut! You're a garbage face. Please, Aunt Carolyn, can I have a bunny? Please?"

"I don't think Conrad and a rabbit would get along too well, Timmy. Rabbits are supposed to be very nervous and you know how crazy Conrad is."

"You could put Conrad in a cage."

"Anyway, your mother already said no. She's the boss, remember?"

"But if you bought me one and just brought it home..."

"Mom would have a fit," Matthew said. "Don't worry, you don't have to buy him a rabbit," he told me. "He always wants a rabbit when we go to a mall and Mom always says no. Anyway, he'll see something else he likes and forget all about a rabbit."

"I will not! I want a rabbit!"

"I don't even know if the mall has a pet store," I said.

"The mall doesn't have a pet store," Matthew said over his shoulder. He was riding up front with me. "Do you want me to stay in the car with the kids when you go into Plymouth's house?" he asked me.

"Well, no. I think you can all come along."

"Don't worry. I'll see that they behave."

They behaved beautifully. Or were they simply shy with the thin woman with the nose ring who answered the door of the big red brick house? The front yard needed weeding, and no one had raked the falling maple leaves, but chimes tinkled on the verandah and an orange cat dozed in the afternoon sunshine.

Plymouth, the woman informed us, was meditating. But would we like to come in? He didn't like to be disturbed but... she would see.

The front room was the kind of space that should have been, and once was, a Victorian parlour cluttered with knick-knacks and photos on the piano, but the high-ceilinged room was bare except for an old green couch and a wooden chest with a bowl of apples sitting on it. An orange and turquoise abstract painting covered one wall and there was a faint smell of curry in the air. Another cat, this one black, gazed at us from the empty hearth.

Allison's kids sat quietly on the couch while I busied myself studying the painting. It was so still I could hear them breathing. They certainly had never seen anything like this. Allison's house was a modern bungalow, a combination of brass lamps, with the cellophane kept on the shades, a worn-out colonial sofa set and a big fake oak coffee table. Joe's gun rack hung over the couch.

Suddenly Plymouth was there, halfway down the stairs before we saw him. He was barefoot and moved like a cat. But he smiled broadly at us, a genuine smile of welcome.

He was wearing a white robe.

I couldn't imagine Johnny here. The place was somehow too ascetic, too monk-like. Too hushed. Too... or was it just that I didn't feel comfortable here myself?

"Just admiring the painting," I said.

"Jane's work," Plymouth explained.

"The woman who answered the door?"

"No, that was Katerina. Jane's no longer with us. Do you like the painting?" he asked me.

"I don't know. It's bright, cheerful..."

"But not restful?"

"Art shouldn't be restful. I'm sorry if we interrupted your meditation. I would have called first but..."

"You thought I wouldn't like to talk on the phone."

"Yes. You're right. You've met Matthew and these are his brothers, Jody and Timmy. We've come to invite you for dinner Friday night. After you left Johnny's place, I invited him, and thought you might like to come along, too. You can see Conrad again, if you're up to it."

"Yes, Conrad. That was most distressing." He shook his head and frowned.

"I don't expect you to shave your beard off. Maybe when he sees you in his own house he'll know you're a friend."

"Let's hope so. Let's hope so. Help yourself to the apples, kids. They haven't been sprayed."

But they didn't want apples, sprayed or not. Maybe it was because they had never seen a man wearing, as Jody said later, "a dress," before.

"I'll do a vegetarian meal," I told Plymouth.

"It's very nice of you to invite me. Can I bring anything?"

Some ginseng wine, perhaps? Pot?

At K-Mart, a Dr. Dreadful kit made Timmy forget all about a rabbit, and Jody wanted a *Homeward Bound* video. Later, Matthew became so engrossed in selecting books at The Bookworm that I left him there to come home later with Peter.

There was a police cruiser parked in front of our place.

But it was only Neil Andersen, having coffee with Allison.

"He just about gave me a heart attack," Allison said. "Honestly.

I thought it was about Joe, laying charges for the truck. I just about died. Opened the door and this OPP cop stands there!"

She seemed in much better spirits. She'd washed her hair and even put some make-up on, although she was still wearing her everlasting sweats.

"I won't keep you," Neil said. "I was just passing by and thought I'd tell you what my mother said. She's talked to the old Russian in the nursing home again, and you'll never guess what happened. No, no more coffee thanks. I've already had three cups, which is one over my daily caffeine intake."

"Neil thinks I should go to this temp agency," Allison reported. "The manager's his neighbour."

"Sure. The money's not great but it's better than nothing."

"And that's about all I've got at this point. Nothing until the child support comes through."

Allison lit a cigarette.

"So tell me about your mother and the old Russian," I prompted.

"Well. The old Russian said there were posters all over Siberia advertising the fact that the Grand Duchess Anastasia was missing. He also said that he knew someone who knew someone else who had actually seen the Grand Duchess after the Romanov massacre. But he didn't believe that Anna Anderson was Anastasia, simply because the real Anastasia, had she survived after her rescue, would have remained hidden!"

"All this royalty stuff," Allison complained. "Just like my mother." Neil ignored her and stared into his empty cup.

"Maybe I will have another cup," he said. "I shouldn't, but I will. This is nuts. I shouldn't even be telling you this, but after my mother talked to this old guy she had a phone call advising her to stay away from him. Someone at the nursing home must have been keeping tabs on him. The only other visitors he's had have been the minister of the Baptist church and an old neighbour."

I poured the coffee. Neil took a big sip and paused before going on.

"This is off the record," he said. "I'm absolutely crazy telling you and this has nothing to do with the investigation, but what my mother said made me think that maybe there's more to this case than meets the eye."

"It wasn't just a crank call?"

"No, it was an authoritative voice, a man's voice. Strange."

"What do you mean there could be more to 'this case' than meets the eye?"

"Well, you were going to talk to Johnny's father about the Romanovs. Someone could have heard about it and gotten there first."

"But I only told our friend Mark, who happens to be Johnny's lawyer. I guess I also told Austin-Wright's neighbour, Mabel McGrath. Peter and Marion knew, naturally, but who would they tell?" Suddenly I thought of Hugh. "Could your father have told anyone?" I asked Allison.

She replied that she didn't concern herself with her mother's "royalty stuff." "With all my problems, I couldn't care less about what Mom and Dad are up to."

"Austin-Wright could have told someone," Neil said.

"His mother," I said. "He told his mother. I know he told his mother and she could have told someone."

"So it wasn't a secret," Neil concluded. "And with the Romanovs in the news again, it could be that someone took a renewed interest in old Austin-Wright. If they kept tabs on an old Russian in a nursing home, it stands to reason that they'd notice Austin-Wright."

"And someone could have planted the gun," I said.

Allison let out a hoot. We were nuts, she said.

But Neil and I looked at each other.

What had seemed so preposterous now seemed entirely possible.

Chapter Thirteen

Allison found work right away as a receptionist at a car dealership, filling in for a woman who'd broken her leg. This meant a mad rush to get the boys registered at school, which she did the same afternoon.

Luckily, the boys would be taking their lunches to school, but someone would have to be there at three-thirty when they came home. Logically, that someone was me.

"I don't blame you if you resent it," Peter said.

"What's the good of resenting it? They're too young to be left alone. If Matthew were a bit older, it would be different. I'll just have to organize things around the kids."

"If you have something to do, an appointment or whatever, they can come to the store."

"It won't be for long, anyway. For one thing, we don't have the room. Allison will have to get an apartment if she stays," I said. "Anyway, I'm getting used to the kids."

That was true. I was especially growing fond of Matthew.

Matthew helped me plan the vegetarian meal for Friday night. To my surprise, he pulled out cookbooks and announced that he would cook the lentil casserole himself. He liked to cook, he said, and his specialty was spaghetti. He could also do bacon and eggs and if pressed, an entire pork-chop dinner. He cooked lots of times, he said, when Allison didn't feel like cooking, or when she slept through the afternoon.

We decided on the lentil casserole, tabouli (which Matthew had never had, but was willing to try), a pasta and almond salad, and squash and apple soup to start with. And, in case the "little kids" didn't like any of this, we'd make a pot of good old macaroni and cheese. Dessert would be opulent: chocolate torte covered with whipped cream and filled with mandarin oranges. Wine for the grown-ups of course, except for Allison, who drank nothing but Labatt's Blue. Juice and ginger ale for the kids. We devised a centrepiece of gourds.

Peter had arranged to have the evening off, and by six-thirty Johnny was sipping beer with Allison, who was in excellent spirits. She loved the car dealership, and on the strength of this job had bought herself three more outfits on credit. The grey skirt and black blazer she wore were a little too matronly, and the red polyester blouse looked cheap, but it was an improvement over the usual sweats. The only other time I had seen Allison in a skirt was at our wedding.

She almost jumped for joy when Johnny said she could come and work for him if she was really stuck. The pay wouldn't be great, but she could use his van, which he wouldn't be able to drive in any case once his impaired driving charge came to court.

But where was Plymouth? By seven, Matthew was worried that the lentil casserole would dry up, and he kept turning the heat on under the soup and turning it off.

"Maybe Plymouth is meditating," Matthew speculated at seven-thirty. "Maybe he forgot."

"I don't know. He's usually pretty good about being somewhere when he says he will," Johnny said. "I guess I should call."

But there was no answer, and at a quarter to eight we finally sat down to eat, although the younger kids had already eaten macaroni and cheese.

Matthew was clearly disappointed. I knew he'd planned to "pick Plymouth's brains."

"Maybe we should go over there," Matthew said, as he filled up on lentils. "Maybe something happened to him."

And over dessert: "Maybe Plymouth fell down and broke his leg."

Johnny telephoned again. No answer.

"We have to go over there," Matthew insisted. He was almost in tears.

"You be quiet," Allison told him. She'd foregone dessert and was having another beer, her fourth, instead. "No one's going there and that's that!"

"But—"

"You're just like your father, always wanting your own way!"

"Maybe someone should check," Johnny said.

"Another murder," Peter said. He hadn't been keen on dining with Plymouth, who, it turned out, he knew from the store. A non-customer who spent hours browsing and had never bought a single book. He was always leaving broadsheets of poetry written by his friends, Peter said. Muriel had taken Plymouth's last batch off the shelf, saying the poems were obscene.

"I'd check myself," Johnny went on, "but I'd like to wait a while. I don't think two beers have put me over, but you never know."

"I'll go," I said. "I'll drive," I told Johnny, "and you can see if he's all right."

"Can I come?" Matthew asked plaintively.

Something told me not to take Matthew along, but Johnny said, "Sure, if it's all right with your mom." Allison, not wanting to harm chances of a job (van included!), agreed that sure, Matthew could go.

Plymouth's house was dark, but his flowered van was parked outside.

"Maybe they all went somewhere," I said. "In another car."

Johnny shook his head. Plymouth was the only one in the house with a vehicle, he said.

"But they often all hang out at the Albion," he said. The Albion was a popular downtown bar. Poetry readings were sometimes held there. "Maybe Plymouth got drunk."

"Drunk?" Matthew piped up. "Plymouth wouldn't get drunk! He meditates."

"It's been known to happen, believe me," Johnny said.

We all stared at the dark house.

"Maybe we should check the Albion," I suggested.

"Better check the house first," Johnny said. He looked worried and suggested I wait in the car with Matthew.

Johnny removed a key from a flower pot and entered the house. The hall light went on. Beside me, Matthew shivered.

Johnny walked slowly when he came out of the house, like an old man, and he was crying. For some reason reminded me of his father.

"What is it? Tell me what's wrong. What happened?"

Johnny kept crying, blubbering like a small child. Finally, he was able to speak.

Plymouth was dead. He had been shot.

Chapter Fourteen

It was the fact that Johnny had been at our house at precisely 6:30 that saved his skin, although he had a few anxious days until the coroner established the time of death. Neighbours had seen Plymouth waving "the hippies" off earlier; they had indeed gone to the Albion for a Friday night drinking spree.

Of course Johnny immediately called Mark, who speculated that perhaps Plymouth knew something Johnny's father had told him, but I think even he realized this theory was coming from the clouds.

There were, it turned out, several suspects: Plymouth's former lover who felt slighted; someone who'd harassed him in a bar; someone Plymouth owed money to. Any of these people could have drifted into the Albion and noticed Plymouth's absence from the group...

"It gets stranger and stranger," Matthew said at the end of that night. The nightmares would come later, but at that point I don't think Plymouth's death had sunk in for him. Matthew had to give a statement, for which Allison had to be present, and she was the one who had hysterics. "Nothing like this ever happens in Meredith! Matthew could have been killed, too!" she yelled at me, as if it were my fault.

I did feel guilty when Matthew said that Plymouth only died because I invited him for dinner. "Otherwise he would have been at the bar with the rest of his friends."

"But there's no connection," I told Peter in bed. "There isn't, is there?"

"Don't be nuts."

"Unless he knew something someone didn't want him to tell me. But what could he have known?"

"He didn't know anything. There's no connection. It was just unlucky timing, that's all."

"I shouldn't have invited him. I just wanted to pick his brains about who could have planted the gun. That's all. Maybe whoever killed him planted the gun in Johnny's van and was afraid that Plymouth knew! That would let Johnny off the hook! Peter, that could be it!"

"No, it's not it. Come off it. They would have killed Johnny before tonight. We should get to sleep."

"You're so insensitive sometimes."

"Where've I heard that before?"

"Well, it's true. Someone I invited for dinner was murdered tonight and you expect me to get to sleep."

He sighed and put his arm around me.

"I'm just saying Plymouth's death has nothing to do with you. That's all."

"Murder follows me around. Johnny's father gets murdered before I can return to talk to him and now Johnny's friend gets shot before he can come to my house for dinner! There could be a connection."

"I think you'll find someone is charged soon for Plymouth's murder," Peter said patiently. And sleepily. Sigh. Sigh. I knew what he was thinking: I should never have gotten involved with Austin-Wright in the first place. And if he was thinking this— but there was no "if"— he *was* thinking this— that meant he thought there was some kind of connection...

I needed to talk to Marion. The problem was that I'd wake up the kids in the living room calling this time of the night.

"Go to sleep," Peter said. "We'll talk in the morning."

But I couldn't sleep. I finally drifted off at four and dreamed about Anna Anderson/Anastasia and Johnny's mother. It was all a jumble about the letters Johnny's mother had, and Austin-Wright was there, too, sitting in front of his wall unit and telling me that the papers were gone. Anastasia replied, "You'll never know." She cackled like a witch.

I awoke, and for a minute she seemed to be in my room, standing at the foot of the bed.

I turned the light on, but of course there was no one there and Peter was sleeping peacefully beside me. I left the light on for the rest of the night.

I decided to take the kids to Emma's the next day. "Good," Allison said. "Get them out of my hair for the afternoon." She was hung over, and still lounging around in her nightie at noon.

It was a fine, sunny, crisp October day and the events of last night seemed distant. "You fell asleep with the light on," Peter remarked at breakfast. I said I'd turned it on to read. I wasn't going to tell anyone about that spooky feeling. I needed fresh air and kids laughing and dogs barking and tea in Emma's kitchen.

"I had a feeling you'd be out today," Emma said, giving me a hug. She seemed cheerful. Mark and Thomas were picking apples, and Allison's kids were only too glad to join them.

"Tell me if you have any plans."

"No plans. We were going to peel apples for the freezer. That's all. You can help. Let me put the kettle on."

The kitchen smelled of the warm bread that was cooling on the counter. Emma spread a cloth for the tea cups and moved over a large vase of autumn leaves.

"So everything's okay?"

"Everything's okay. I haven't heard from you-know-who again. But how about you? That was awful last night."

"You're telling me. I would have invited you for dinner, but frankly we were crowded as it was."

"How's that going, with your sister-in-law there?"

I pulled a face and sighed dramatically. "What can you do? Family. She'll have to find a place of her own if she stays in Guelph."

"No chance of reconciling with hubby?" Emma poured tea.

"I have a feeling she'll go back to him, but not yet. I'm enjoying the kids though, especially Matthew."

"He's the oldest, isn't he?"

I nodded. "Did Mark tell you Matthew was there last night?"

"Yeah. But kids are adaptable. He'll think more about it twenty years from now than he does now, I think. He'll be telling his therapist."

We looked out of the window. Thomas and the younger kids were throwing apples to the dogs but Matthew was talking to Mark. Probably discussing conspiracy plots, I thought. But I didn't say this aloud, because Emma suddenly looked unhappy, as if she realized that bright and articulate Matthew was conversing with Mark in a way that Thomas never did. Emma sighed and I changed the subject to talk about Plymouth.

"The murder probably had something to do with him being gay. Or it was about drugs. Guelph might be filled with the Greenpeace crowd, but it's still the same old conservative place underneath. 'The Royal City,' as they used to call it. It makes me miss Holland," Emma said.

Did she ever think of going back there with Thomas? I wondered, as Mark, followed by dogs and kids, carried in a big basket of apples. Conrad darted through his legs, almost upsetting him, and snatched an apple.

"No! No!" But it was pointless to protest, because the apple was already down his gullet. Conrad grinned at me. "Sorry about that," I told Mark. "Did I tell you that Scottie's going to give Conrad a lesson in not eating forbidden food? Forbidden fruit, in this case. We have to play bridge with them in return."

"Them being Scottie and Mother?" Emma laughed.

"What's with Scottie's job?" I asked Mark.

"He's on the short list. We'll be deciding this week." Mark heaved the basket onto the counter. As he did so, several apples tumbled to the floor. This time Kelly was a culprit, too.

We finally had to lock the dogs out of the house because their ongoing drooling and dribbling as they salivated over apple cores and peel soon created a puddle on the floor. Emma and I peeled and sliced, while Mark, the chauvinist, drank tea and talked. He repeated Emma's theory about Plymouth's murder, but he was plainly not interested in any aspect of this last grisly affair, since Johnny was obviously not involved.

Mark was soon back to the Romanovs. Matthew had slinked in from outside and he was not bashful about adding his input. Matthew thought for sure that a Romanov agent had killed Mr. Austin-Wright, and he also stated, very seriously, that he was "utterly, five thousand per cent convinced" that the same people could have done Plymouth in, too.

"I doubt that very much, pal," Mark said. "If these Romanov people went after anyone else it would be Johnny, don't you think?"

"Not if they knew Johnny didn't know anything."

"Maybe they'll go after Johnny's mother," I said, "with her valuable papers. And what about those papers, Mark?" This was what I really wanted to ask him.

"I'm seeing Marlies next week," Mark said. "She's one tough customer, but I think I've made her think twice about peddling her papers. But I doubt if she has anything. Still, it'll be interesting to see what she does have."

"What papers?" Matthew wanted to know.

"I don't think this is a suitable conversation." Emma looked pointedly at Matthew. "We have some videos if you want to watch them," she told Matthew. "Or you could play with the computer."

Matthew asked if they were on the Internet. They weren't. Reluctantly, with much sighing, he took himself off to the living room. A few minutes later the front door slammed.

"What I don't understand," I told Mark, "is why you've let so much time go by about those papers."

"Marlies wouldn't talk to me, is why."

"You're representing her son on a murder charge, and she won't talk to you?"

"I told you, she's tough. Her husband's been insisting everything goes through him, but my secretary finally got through to Marlies."

"I wouldn't mind seeing those papers myself," I said. "And I know Marion would be interested, too. If you do get them, what's the chance of seeing them, or at least finding out what's in them?"

"I seem to remember you saying the Romanov angle was nuts." Mark raised an eyebrow.

I thought of last night's spooky dream and shivered. It had been so real. Sitting in Emma's comfortable, sunny kitchen which smelled now of McIntosh apples, I knew in a way I had not known before that Johnny had not killed his father.

"Neil Andersen, the OPP officer who was on duty the night Johnny's father was killed, dropped in on me recently," I found myself saying. "His mother in Saskatchewan knows this ancient man in a nursing home who's Russian. He was in Siberia when the Romanovs were shot. He heard from someone who heard from someone that Anastasia had really gotten away. After this old guy told Andersen's mother what he knew, she received a phone call from someone telling her to leave the man alone."

"Maybe some relative who didn't want the old man bothered," Emma suggested, scooping up apple peels and putting them in the compost bucket.

"He doesn't have any relatives," I said. "And no close friends. He's outlived everyone."

"So now we'll have a murder in a nursing home out west," Emma said matter-of-factly.

"Are you talking about that cop who came to your house?" an eager voice asked. We hadn't heard Matthew coming back in. "Are they going to get that guy, too? Johnny should look out, that's what I think!"

I tossed an apple peel at Matthew and asked him if he didn't know that children should only speak when they were spoken to.

But what if he were right? I thought, as he ducked and stuck his tongue out at me.

Chapter Fifteen

By the time Peter and I went to play cards at Scottie and Mabel's, Matthew had had two nightmares, waking up in the middle of the night and crying. He sleepwalked once, which an exasperated Allison said he'd also done when he was four years old.

To distract him, I was tempted to take him with us, but Peter and Allison disagreed, Peter because he wanted to get away from Allison's family, and Allison because it was a school night.

Now that the kids were in school, they were all sleeping in the guest room, two on the bed, and one in a sleeping bag on the floor. Allison camped out on the living room couch, from where she watched TV, specifically call-in psychic shows until late at night. This worried Peter: what if she used our telephone to seek advice at $6.00 a minute about her future?

Joe had called three times, but only to talk to the kids, whom he instructed to tell their mother that he loved her and missed her. The younger ones seemed unaffected by their father's voice, but Matthew appeared sad, and once it looked as if he'd been crying in the bathroom.

As a result of Joe's calls, Allison was wondering if she should go back to Meredith. "What should I do? I don't know what to do!"

She had even called her mother for advice and an update. Marion said Joe was driving around in his truck with a hang-dog look on his face, and that Joe's mother had said he was so upset he wasn't eating.

"It's just that I was with him so long," Allison bleated to Peter.

Peter said: "If you want to go home, go home. It's your life."

What Scottie did was simple. He placed tidbits and treats, bits of bologna, and dog cookies in his field, and attached Conrad's choke collar and lead. "No!" was followed by a quick, sharp pop, not as dramatic in execution as the trainer's at Puppy Kindergarten, but enough to make Conrad pay attention.

And, ultimately, to obey. Watching from the driveway with Mabel and Peter, at first I was afraid Conrad was going to choke, so eager was he to swallow whatever morsel came his way. But Scottie persisted, and by the time they'd made the rounds five times, Conrad was only making token efforts to retrieve the treats. Each resist earned a word of praise from Scottie.

"Your turn now," Scottie said, handing me the lead.

I knew I couldn't do it. It was growing dark, but I could make out the gleam in Conrad's eyes as Scottie handed the lead over. Here's Mom, the old softie. At last I get my treats!

Conrad was away before I even got a grip on the lead, flying off to the first treat, which he devoured at once, grinning back at me over his shoulder.

"No! No!" Scottie was at his side and grabbed him by the scruff of the neck, shaking him. "No, No! Bad dog! No!" Conrad's tail went between his legs.

"I'll just walk along with you, then. Let's try it again. He's a stubborn one, all right."

Conrad was an angel, a frightened one, with Scottie by my side. He did try to eat, but Scottie's look, rather than my "pop," stopped him. "Good boy! Good boy! Good Conrad!"

"That's it, that's it," Scottie murmured in approval, and when we were done, Scottie gave me a treat, which I presented to Conrad. While he ate, though, he gazed longingly at the field with its gourmet treasures.

We left Conrad in the car while we played cards. To my surprise, Mabel had set up a card table in the living room, which I'd never seen before. The green sofa and chairs looked new, as did the tables with the brass trim and glass lamps, but the floral wallpaper was old and faded. The large picture of Edinburgh Castle over the couch and a small pile of magazines on a stand were the only personal touches. There had been a fireplace once, but it was boarded over. A floor-model television, with a ship's model on the top, stood in a corner.

Mabel had set out dishes of peanuts and chocolate-covered raisins, and Scottie produced a bottle of Scotch.

"Nothing like a wee dram on a chilly autumn night, wouldn't you say now?" Scottie asked.

"Oh, stop talking like Robbie Burns, Humphrey," Mabel said. But this was said with a titter and a grin and she accepted the drink Scottie passed her.

Scottie ignored her and raised his glass in a toast.

"Here's to dogs, the best of God's creatures!"

Mabel and Scottie played against Peter and me. Mother and son were excellent bridge players, and as the evening progressed and the Scotch flowed, even Peter seemed to be enjoying himself. We hadn't played bridge in years, not since we used to play with Marion and Hugh, and Mabel and Scottie easily won the first two rubbers. Mabel was especially good, bidding six no trump and easily making it, despite Scottie's in-held breath. Mabel seemed to enjoy her drinks, and didn't protest when Scottie refilled his shot glass over and over.

"Now this is what I call a fine evening," Scottie said, as we started the third rubber. "A few tots, cards, and lunch to follow. It does make for a fine evening!"

"I hope you haven't gone to any trouble," I told Mabel, although I was getting hungry. We'd only picked up pizza slices on the way so we could get to their place before dark.

"She's got quite the spread, Mother has," Scottie said. "Lovely sandwiches and pickles. Pie, too, if I'm not mistaken. Isn't that right, Mother?"

"Play your cards, Humphrey," Mabel told him, but she seemed pleased by his accolades, and when he went on fondly about the pies and scones she baked, she hardly protested at all.

"Any fool can make scones. What're you bidding, Humphrey?"

"Three spades."

Peter passed. Mabel raised to four spades. I passed.

"Five spades!" Scottie cried.

They went down on that hand, which was the occasion for the filling of the shot glass again.

Peter and I bid three no-trump and made it, went down again, but won two games in a row, which gave us a rubber at last.

We had our lunch in the kitchen. Mabel thriftily turned off the living room lights behind us. Scottie lugged in the Scotch bottle and refilled glasses while Mabel made the tea. She set out egg and ham salad sandwiches, cut-glass dishes of pickles, olives and carrot sticks, and an apple pie with a shiny, golden, sugared crust. She used her good china cups, and glass plates with a golden rim on them for the sandwiches.

Scottie, by this time, was, in his own words, "happy," and he called Lady, who'd been dozing by the stove, to his side. The old dog limped as she came over. Arthritis, Mabel explained. The damp weather bothered Lady.

Over tea, the talk naturally was of dogs, with Scottie reminiscing about the first dog he had ever owned, Tim, back in Scotland, when he was "a wee lad" of seven. "Do you remember, Mother..." Tim had walked all over the town by himself, stopping for treats at the butcher's and the baker's. Everyone had known Tim, a little white-and-black Border Collie, apparently abandoned by gypsies, and shot by mistake by a farmer. Tim couldn't work, but Mabel had taken him for her boy, and the dog had lived to the age of eighteen.

"We waited for our Tim to pass on before we emigrated," Scottie said, which led to talk of Scotland and coming to Canada. They'd lived in New Brunswick for a year, where Mabel had a cousin, but work was hard to find, and they'd come to Ontario, first to Toronto, and then to Guelph.

"You must miss Scotland," I told Mabel.

"Not any more. I miss the sea. We were right on the coast, but I knew there would be more opportunity in Canada, which I always wanted to see as a girl." Gur-r-l, she pronounced it.

"You haven't been back? Peter's parents went to England a couple of years ago."

"I'm sending Mother back if I get that job with the Board," Scottie said. "Maybe I'll go, too, if we can find someone to look after the mutts."

Mabel frowned at him. "Humphrey's applied for a position with the Board of Education," she told me after a second. "Nothing, however, has been decided as of yet." She gave Scottie another look, and if he hadn't been in his cups, he likely would have shut up, but Scottie prattled on quite happily. The Board job would be easy street, none of this union hall hiring business, and our lawyer friend was putting in a good word.

"Then it's off to Scotland we go!" He threw Lady a piece of egg sandwich.

"Get the job first and then we'll talk about Scotland," Mabel said. "Scotland's the last thing on my mind now. With the way the union's treating you, I'm more concerned about keeping a roof over our heads."

"Things are not that bad, Mother," Scottie said. "Off to Scotland is what I say!"

Scottie was still talking when we left at eleven-thirty, and he staggered as he walked us to the car. "Tally-ho then, auf wiedersehen, and cheerio!" He thumped the fender of the Volvo and woke up Conrad, who began barking and jumping. "Tootle-loo then! Until we meet again!"

"We'll have to invite them some time," I told Peter on the way home.

"I bet he'd rather we went to his place. Old Scottie won't be able to throw back the whiskey if he has to drive. I'm surprised his mother lets him drink so much."

"I think she likes a drink herself. You know what? I had a good time."

"Not bad," Peter agreed. "For a change. They're quite the couple."

"Scottie seems happy enough living with his mother. But I can't see him bringing a woman home, can you?"

"What woman would want part of that arrangement?"

"I like Mabel, though. She reminds me of Millicent. I bet Millicent would have liked her." Although born in Canada, Millicent had been very Scottish.

"We should fix Allison up with Scottie," Peter mused. "Lots of room for the boys out there. Dogs to play with. Mabel to boss everyone around."

"Everyone but Allison. And Mabel wouldn't let her smoke, I bet. So that would be the end of that. Unless Allison insisted on moving out. With Scottie, of course, and where do you think they'd end up but at our place?"

"I'd move in with Mabel," Peter said. "How much longer do you think Allison's going to stay?"

"Who knows?"

"She's been drinking too much. I bet there won't be any of that six pack left."

But Peter was wrong. One bottle remained, and Allison was snoring on the couch.

Chapter Sixteen

It was with astonishment that I found the kids still at home when I surfaced at ten the next morning. "It's a PD day!" Jody informed me gleefully. Allison, of course, had left for work. At least she'd set out cereal for them, but they were all still in their pyjamas and watching *Oprah*.

Damn Allison, I thought, making coffee. I had a slight headache from last night's imbibing, and I knew Peter too had overslept. He'd probably flown out of the house, assuming the kids would be going to school.

"I guess Mom forgot to tell you about the PD day," Matthew sighed as he came into the kitchen. Conrad was right behind. Matthew set a half-empty cereal bowl on the floor for Conrad to slurp from.

"Yeah, I guess she did forget."

"I can look after the kids if you have to do something." He sat down at the table.

"I don't think so, Matthew."

"I babysat in Meredith all the time. If Mom had to go somewhere or they went out Saturday night."

"It's okay, Matthew." I forced myself to smile. It wasn't his fault, and I didn't have anything planned for the day, but Allison could at least have checked with me. "Why don't you guys get dressed and then we'll figure out what to do this afternoon?"

He began gathering the rest of the breakfast dishes. Conrad barked. "Should I let him lick out the others?"

"They go in the dishwasher anyway."

"Dad called last night and talked to Mom." He put another bowl down for Conrad. "He wants her to come back but she said, 'No way, Jose.' But then she began crying and I bet she'll end up going back."

That explained all the beer, I thought. Peter had pointedly left the empties out, but Allison had put them away in the morning. I hoped she had a doozer of a hangover.

"Dad said life was empty without all of us there," Matthew went on. "Mom called Gram, too."

"Did you talk to your grandmother?"

"Uh-uh. Mom sent us to bed but I wasn't asleep."

"This isn't much fun for you, is it?" I passed him Allison's ashtray. The coffee was ready. Matthew got me a mug from the cupboard and milk from the fridge. He poured out my coffee and made a face as he dumped cigarette butts into the garbage. That was another thing: Allison's constant smoking.

"It's okay." He sat down opposite me and considered my question. He reminded me so much of Peter right then, serious and— what was the word?— old-fashioned? Reserved but somehow vulnerable— the very qualities that had attracted me to Peter in the first place fifteen years before. I'd just broken up with a live-in filmmaker when I met Peter at The Bookworm, where I'd gone to autograph some of my cookbooks. He called me "Miss Archer" and did not even kiss me on our first date.

"But sometimes when I wake up I think I'm still in Meredith," Matthew went on. "Then it's strange when I know I'm in Guelph. But it's okay. The school's bigger, though."

"But it's all right?" The coffee tasted great, but my head was beginning to pound.

Matthew shrugged. "There's this guy, Eddy, who wants me to come over and play games on his computer."

It hadn't occurred to me to buy some computer games for the kids. I'd have to do that.

"You'll have to take him up on it. And you tell me what games you like and I'll buy them and you can invite Eddy back. I think I'm going to get an aspirin, Matthew."

"Do you have a hangover, too? Mom had a splitting head this morning."

"Why don't you help your brothers get out of their PJs?"

"You could lie down if you want. I can keep the kids quiet."

"That's okay, Matthew. I'll be fine. Just see to your brothers and I'll get myself an aspirin."

But my bed looked pretty comfortable as I swallowed a pill in the bathroom. However, however— damn Allison! I'd have to do something with the kids in the afternoon, I thought, as I stepped into the shower. Marion had been so right: Allison was one to take advantage of you. And what if I'd really had something planned for this afternoon? I'd have had to cancel because of the kids. While the hot water splashed over me I delivered the lecture I'd never be brave enough to give Allison in person. You inconsiderate bitch, what makes you think you can just waltz into my life and take it over? What makes you assume I'm here just for you, for your convenience?

I could imagine her startled face changing to sullen fury as she gathered bags and baggage for a return to Meredith. Phoning Marion, phoning Peter. Phoning Joe? Flying out of the house, yelling...

Peter would be aghast. He might complain about Allison, but that was all right: she was his sister.

"You silly, selfish woman," I muttered as I towelled myself dry.

By the time I was dressed, all the kids were dressed, too, and Matthew had not only stacked the dishwasher but started it. He'd picked up the living room and informed me he'd begun a wash because "the kids" were running out of clothes. Allison had meant to do a wash last night, but "with the phone calls and all" she'd forgotten about it.

And how about if he made everyone grilled cheese sandwiches for lunch?

The phone rang. Mark.

"We're going to London this afternoon! After considerable threats and arm twisting, Her Highness Marlene Dietrich has agreed that we can look at some of her priceless documents today! I just got off the phone with the bitch."

"Sorry, Mark. No can do." I told him about it being a PD day and my predicament.

"No problem. Thomas is off, too. We'll take all the kids out to my place. Emma won't mind."

I looked at Matthew, who was cutting bread. I knew he'd expected to be with me all day and I felt disappointed on his behalf.

And anyway, why shouldn't Emma mind? I thought, and said so.

"Hell, she'll be glad. The kids'll get Thomas out from under so she can work on her hangings. Someone just phoned from Arizona with a commission. She's in seventh heaven."

"All the more reason not to impose on her."

Matthew looked at me sharply. He was disappointed.

"I could go tomorrow," I said.

"Tomorrow's no good. It's today or nothing. They're off to see her husband's uncle in Montreal tomorrow."

We could take Matthew with us, I thought.

But then Emma wouldn't have Matthew to keep an eye on things.

"I'm not going unless I discuss this with Emma first. Why do I have to come along anyway?"

"Because Marlene Dietrich says so, that's why."

"Let me call Emma."

Matthew fixed the sandwiches while I made the phone call.

"Of course I don't mind." She sounded quite happy. What she really wanted to talk about was the commission. The tourists who had bought her hangings had shown them at a community centre where this artist was giving a class. "And she fell in love with my work! Can you believe it? She spent some time in Canada, up north, and loves anything Canadian. She wants something to do with nature, but what I actually do is up to me. Mark says we should drive down there when the hanging's done. We haven't had a real vacation for a long time."

"Well, Emma— wow! That's great!"

"She also said maybe she could get me some workshops down there! She teaches this class for people who want to create from their lives— collages and things like that. I could do the same thing with fabric art, she says.

"So you bring the kids here and don't worry about a thing!"

Matthew took the news with grace, but I could tell that he was disappointed. I explained as best as I could. "Actually, I'd love to take you with me because you've been such a help in the past, but this is lawyer's business. I don't think the woman we're going to see likes kids too much, and as she's showing Mark and me some letters that could very well help with Johnny's defence. It's important."

"I know. It's okay."

He began frying the cheese sandwiches.

"I'll call Peter and he'll come and get you. He can pick up a pizza for supper. Maybe you can even go out."

If only I had taken Matthew with me.

The great thing about going anywhere with Mark was that you didn't have to talk much because he did it all. A few years before, when he'd had to interview someone in North Bay, he gave me a ride to Meredith and I don't think I got in two words the entire way because he was so riled up about the provincial election.

I was glad to put my head back and close my eyes. Neither the pill nor Matthew's grilled cheese sandwich had helped my headache.

My temples were pounding before we even reached the 401. I doubt if Mark noticed my monosyllabic responses.

"Someone had to clue Anna Anderson in on the Russian court. Did you know the Soviets had agents watching Kerensky, head of the provisional government in Russia in 1917, until he died in California as an old man? Someone had to give Anderson the information she had. She couldn't have learned everything by hanging around with the Russian emigrés. Mind you, she made mistakes and her supporters explained these away by saying rifle butt blows to the head had impaired her memory. They also said that was partly why she had lost the use of the Russian language."

"Uh-huh."

"Can you imagine the gall, the nerve, to pass yourself off as a Russian Grand Duchess and not be able to speak the language? People said she understood it, but answered in German. And that she spoke Russian in her sleep, but it was probably really Polish. German nurses and servants wouldn't have known the difference. Speaking some Polish, she would be able to understand Russian, but not to speak it."

"Really."

"So she'd let out a single Russian word or isolated phrase and bingo! her supporters said she knew Russian. That she could speak it if she really wanted to. And they attributed her stubbornness to proof of her identity. An impostor would be falling over backwards trying to impress everyone, but Anderson just went her own merry way, being herself, which was the best strategy whether she knew it or not.

"She had this emphatic personality that drew people in, these fantastic blue eyes that reminded everyone of the Tsar. I think the Soviets got to her later, though. In the beginning she made the most appalling mistakes. In 1922 she said she had come from Paris to Berlin, because a newspaper article claimed Anastasia had been there. Only when the Paris thing turned out to be false, did she talk about having come to Berlin via Romania. She said her husband, Alexander Tchaikovsky, the man she claimed rescued her at Ekaterinburg and who took her to Romania, got her wearing this apparatus that altered her features, her nose and lips. Her lips were too big, you see, and her nose had a tilt to it.

"Of course she had her teeth removed at the insane asylum to alter her appearance. She said it was because her teeth pained her from the rifle butt blows, but some nurses admitted Miss Unknown said she wanted to change her appearance.

"People talked about her having some teeth out, but no one later ever mentioned the miraculous face cover that altered her nose and lips, apparently. But it's there all right, in the old books. And then she ran way."

"Is that right?" I knew about her running away, but I didn't want to discuss this, or anything else, right then.

"Yup, right after she moved in with the noble Russian family in 1922. Just took off. Later, Franziska's former landlady's daughter said Franziska had returned to her place when she ran away. They even found the clothes Franziska had left there, clothes the Russians had bought her. And get this. The landlady and the patient from the asylum who first suggested Franziska might be a Russian Grand Duchess knew each other.

"It's just incredible how Franziska pulled it off. She always came through. No matter who had evidence against her, her supporters remained loyal. Not only because she resembled the Romanovs, and not only because of her regal bearing, but because of what she knew! And someone had to have told her, because if head injuries incurred at Ekaterinburg destroyed much of her memory, what was she doing knowing insignificant details like the colour of her mother's dress in a black-and-white photograph? Someone had to tell her. And guess who that was?"

"Who?"

"The Soviets, of course, who wanted to keep the Romanov family divided and the crazy monarchists running all over the place. I have a feeling that the Russians are behind this. With all this talk of burying the Tsar in St. Petersburg and interest in the monarchy, Anderson still rankles. There's something behind all this, I'll tell you that."

I fell asleep.

Mark did not notice. I kept coming to, hearing "Romanov" and "Anastasia" and "Russia," and dozing off again. The cloudy fall weather added to my sleepiness. This part of southern Ontario is known as the snow belt, and it wasn't hard to imagine snow coming from the heavy fall sky and covering the road and fields. My headache was getting worse and all I could think of was my own warm bed and a cold cloth on my head.

By the time we came to the first cut-off for London, I was feeling distinctly ill.

"Mark, I'm going to have to stop and have a coffee. My head is coming right off."

"I didn't know you were sick. Why didn't you say something?"

"I'm not sick. I just have a headache. We played cards with Mabel and Scottie last night and I think I drank too many of Scottie's wee drams. I hope I have some aspirin with me. Damn. My headache wasn't too bad until we started driving."

"We'll stop and buy some aspirin if you don't have any." He looked impatient as he turned into the parking lot of a doughnut shop. I knew he was hoping I wouldn't ruin the session with Johnny's mother, and I saw him glancing at his watch as I fumbled in my purse for the pills. I didn't find any. Luckily there was a strip mall with a drugstore in it just down the road. I closed my eyes while Mark went into the pharmacy.

In the doughnut shop I went into the Ladies' and splashed cold water on my face. I looked wretched. My hair was sticking to the back of my head from resting against the seat and my face was flushed. I had not only forgotten the aspirin but a hairbrush as well. The best I could do was to run my fingers through my hair to fluff it up.

Suddenly the room swam and I had to hold onto the vanity. Groping for the wall, I made my way to a cubicle, where I sat with my head between my knees. I thought I was going to be sick to my stomach, and all I could think was: better now, better here than to throw up all over the white carpet at Johnny's mother's house.

And then I was sick.

Mercifully I no longer felt faint, but my face was mottled, my eyes bleary. I splashed and splashed water on my face, but I knew I still looked like an absolute wretch as I staggered back to the front of the doughnut shop.

Mark was leafing through the *Toronto Sun* and looking at his watch.

"I ordered you a coffee, but it's probably cold by now. We should get going. We're supposed to be there in twenty minutes and I don't know my way around north London."

The aspirin container sat by my cup. My headache had gone to my right temple, which throbbed in a far-off kind of way. I knew if I drank the coffee that I'd be sick again. I pushed the cup away.

"You okay?"

"I'll live through it."

"I didn't know Scottie drank so much. Aren't you going to take your aspirin?"

"I don't think it's such a hot idea to put anything in my stomach right now. Maybe you could stop for some breath mints or some-thing. And Scottie doesn't drink that much. We were just there playing cards after Scottie gave Conrad a lesson in not eating off the ground."

I followed Mark out of the doughnut shop.

"What difference does it make if Scottie drinks or not? Is he getting that job?"

"It's down to him and a young guy just out of apprenticeship. I'm doing my best but it's not just me."

At the drugstore I asked Mark to buy me a cheap hairbrush along with the breath freshener. I knew he was nervous about being late for our appointment— it would be like Marlies to go out if we were a few minutes late— but I didn't care. I leaned back and closed my eyes and wished I could rent a motel room while Mark went to interview Marlies on his own.

The cellular phone rang while a frowning Mark was just coming out of the drugstore.

It was Emma. A frantic, distraught Emma, weeping and crying.

Thomas and Matthew had disappeared.

Chapter Seventeen

Mark was not sympathetic.

"Oh, for crying out loud, Em, they're probably down the road or in the woodlot. We're just on our way to see Johnny's mother. What do you expect me to do about it from London?"

Emma hung up. Mark shook his head and when the phone rang again, he passed it to me.

"Carolyn. Oh, Carolyn. Jensen took them. I know he did. He phoned right after you dropped the kids off and said he knew there wasn't any school today. And then I saw this blue car driving back and forth. A rental car because it had that shiny sticker. Jody and Timmy were still playing with Conrad and Kelly but Matthew and Thomas..."

"Call the police, Emma." Mark looked up from his directions to
Marlies' house and gave me an are-you-crazy look. "You have to call
the police, right now!"

I hadn't even phoned Allison to tell her where her kids were
spending the afternoon, I realized.

Emma couldn't stop crying.

"But why take both of them?" I asked.

"Because Jensen wouldn't know which one was his son!"

"But how could he take both of them?"

"Maybe there was someone in the car with him! Even if he knew
who Thomas was they couldn't leave Matthew, could they? Tell
Mark he has to come home right now! Explain it to him! I want
Mark to come home!"

This crazy, stunning news should have sent my headache pack-
ing, as in stories where someone becomes sober at the moment of
danger, but I spent most of the return trip to Guelph lying in the back
seat of Mark's car, unable to concentrate on anything but my
pounding head. After the initial shock of learning that Jensen had
re-surfaced, Mark, for once, was grim and silent. Somewhere in my
head, away from the pain, I knew I should talk to Mark about Emma's
worries— it was time someone did— but the effort of opening my
mouth and speaking was too great.

I listened to the low hum of Mark's voice as he talked to Emma.
There was no news. Matthew and Thomas had not been found, nor
had there been any sighting of the blue rental car. At some point,
Mark called his buddies at the Guelph Police Station and learned that
Customs at the airport and all border crossings had been alerted.

It was almost dark when at last we pulled into Mark's driveway.
All the lights were on and I saw our Volvo, as well as another car.
"Jeez, my mother's here," Mark said.

Mrs. Richman answered the door.

"I have never heard of such a thing! The reporters heard it on the police scanner and contacted me, of all things!"

Her usually pristine face was flushed, but she wore pearls and a sweater, as if she had just come from a tea. Behind her, other faces seemed to wave and flow before my eyes: Peter, shocked; Allison, beyond shock and hysteria; Timmy and Jody, scared and silent. Emma's face was hidden in the cushions of the couch.

"I have just telephoned the doctor for your wife," Mrs. Richman told Mark. "You had better make a phone call to the papers, so that this situation does not make it into print."

I fainted.

When I came to, it seemed to be the middle of the night. My headache was gone. I was on Thomas' bed and Emma was sitting in the rocking chair I remembered her buying at a flea market the previous year. She'd sanded it down, but had never gotten around to refinishing it...

Matthew, I thought.

Thomas.

"There's tea on the night table," Emma said softly. "I just brought it in so it's still hot. And some biscuits."

I sat up to sip the tea. I didn't have to ask her if there was any news. I could tell from her drained face that the boys had not been found.

"The doctor looked at you when he was here. He said you might have had an allergic reaction to the Scotch. The doctor left valium if you want some."

I shook my head.

"I sent Mark's mother home. I couldn't stand it any more." She got up, wobbled, but steadied herself. "I'll tell Peter you're awake. He wanted to sit with you, but Allison's been in a pretty bad state."

Peter was with me in a minute. Without a word, he lay beside me and put his arms around me.

Somewhere a pot rattled, but then the house was still. Child-find, I thought. Missing children. I tried to imagine never seeing Matthew again, never knowing if he was alive or dead. I would always wait for him to ring the doorbell, I realized, and tried to imagine his fright and terror as strangers drove him away. Would they kill him, I wondered, when they realized which boy was which? Would he struggle, comply with their demands? He was a smart boy. Maybe he would outsmart them. Escape.

He was a smart boy. He would outsmart them.

But he was just a little boy. What could he do?

It was a long night. I was aware that Emma kept coming into the room to check and once I thought I saw Mark, who looked as if he'd been crying. I could smell whiskey on his breath. The phone rang. I clung to Peter. I slept and dreamed of Allison's house in Meredith, of Matthew flicking on the remote control of the television. Flick, flick, the channels changed, gun fights interspersed with scenes from *Homeward Bound*. "You'll never see me again," Matthew said sadly. "No," I said. "You have to come home." The television said that Matthew was missing. It's only a dream, a voice in the dream said.

I thought I was still dreaming when I awoke to the sound of Marion's voice. But it was no dream. She and Hugh had driven straight down from up north and arrived at three in the morning. Marion was distraught, but she had packed Emma and Mark off to bed and was cooking breakfast. I was shocked that I was ravenous.

The first thing I did was apologize to Allison.

"I should have told you where your kids were."

Allison opened her mouth to say something, but her mother cut her off.

"And she should have advised you the kids would be home all

day and not at school," Marion said, setting toast in front of me. "It wasn't your fault, Carolyn."

"Has anyone told Joe?" Peter wanted to know. "Someone should tell him."

"He's off hunting, but Hugh's sent someone after him. I'm sure he'll get here as soon as he can," Marion said.

We didn't have to ask where Hugh was. His snores filled the house, emanating from the living room where he was asleep on the couch. Jody and Timmy were watching television in the same room, but the noise didn't wake him.

Without a word, Allison took her plate and went into the living room.

The strange night was followed by a strange day. Mark was up by ten. Pacing and pacing. He kicked the dogs outside and no one objected. The police came and installed a bug on the telephone. An unmarked police car sat on the road. Mark fielded reporters' calls: "We're hopeful and waiting." The television station called, wanting to send their people so Emma and Allison could make a public plea. Hugh took the dogs for a run, accompanied by Timmy and Jody. Allison smoked and smoked, but no one complained. Emma remained closeted in her room.

After the dishes were put away, Marion worked on her knitting. The orange cat, Pumpkin, slept by her feet, and for once, when Hugh let the dogs in after their run, they did not harass the cat.

The police brought us pizza. Timmy and Jody complained about the green peppers.

The OPP brought out their dogs, but the male ran off because a farmer down the road had a bitch in heat.

There was no word from Joe.

"Emma wants to see you," Mark told me. He was drinking again.

I thought: How far away the Romanov business now seems, how unimportant. He avoided my eyes, but he walked me to the bedroom.

Emma looked as if she could not cry any more. Her face had ballooned with the shed tears. Without her mascara, her eyes seemed to have disappeared.

"When all this is over I think Mark and I are going to split up."

I sat on the floor. If Emma had been a touching kind of person, I would have taken her hand, but she's almost always been reserved in a physical sense.

"You're just upset. It'll work out. You'll see."

"You don't know," she said. "You don't know everything, but I told Mark and he didn't like what he heard."

"He's upset, too. You should have seen him driving back here as fast as he could. He was out of his mind with worry."

"I don't think he wants all this hassle. He just wants a quiet, normal life."

"None of this is your fault. At least the stuff with Jensen is out in the open now." I didn't say that perhaps none of this would have happened if she'd told Mark Jensen was bothering her earlier. "And think how far back you and Mark go. He never got over you after you left."

"He would have married that lawyer if I hadn't turned up. I know he regrets not doing so now."

"You don't know that. Did he tell you that?"

"He didn't have to. But I know. At least I'll be rid of his mother."

"Emma— "

"I told Mark everything. Everything. Listen, you don't know everything. You don't know what Jensen said he'd tell Mark if I didn't let him have Thomas."

"You don't have to tell me."

"No, no, I want to. Do you know why Jensen wants Thomas? He's married to this woman who can't have kids. She's also very religious, one of those fundamentalist types." Emma made a face. "You know that I know what that's like. And what he has over me, not only to tell Mark but my parents as well... It'll kill them. They'll hate me."

She wept again, and now I did take her hand, but after a moment she pulled free.

"What Jensen has over me is that he knows I had a lesbian relationship for a little while in Holland," she said simply. "It turned him on way back when, but now it's a different story. It's a different story for Mark, too."

"Oh, Emma. A lot of people have experimented. I can't imagine Mark would want to get rid of you for that. And so long ago."

"An ex-lesbian wife, an adopted son he can't stand. Jensen even said he'd tell Mark's mother!"

"Jensen's not going to be telling anyone anything when they find him. And they will find him, I know they will!"

"They could be anywhere by now."

"Jensen wouldn't harm his own son. And why should he hurt Matthew? He'll probably leave Matthew somewhere once he finds out which boy is his son."

"Jensen said he and his wife had prayed and prayed for a baby and then the Lord told them to look after the son he had!"

I waited for her to stop crying. Or not to stop. Whatever Emma did was okay with me. Her story filled me with sadness for her and with disgust for Mark, who was so much more rigid than I had ever imagined.

At last she pulled herself together and said that if Thomas was found, she was taking him back to Holland.

"You and I have to have a talk," I told Mark. He gazed at me warily, trying to gauge how much I knew. I think the look in my eye told him I knew everything, and he certainly wasn't going to let anyone overhear our conversation. He got his jacket. I recovered my coat from the hall closet where someone, Marion probably, had hung it, and we went outside.

He gave a half-wave to the police car and we walked to the back of the property, over to the woodlot. He kept his head down and I knew he was prepared for what I had to say.

"You are an absolute shit, Mark. All that baloney about the common man and doing your own thing, and you're as straightlaced as any suit I've ever met. An absolute shit. Just because of what Emma did years and years ago, you want to call it quits."

"I didn't say that." His voice was quiet.

"You didn't say much, did you?"

"I was surprised, that's all. It's been a nervous day."

I picked up a branch and threw it with all my might.

"You should be in there comforting her instead of acting like some eighty-year-old Conservative-appointee judge! As I said, an absolute shit!"

He took it. He poked the earth with his toe and hung his head while I went on: he made me sick, he was an inconsiderate chauvinist, and more of the same. He just kept poking at the earth.

Suddenly the dogs were there, jumping and barking. I threw a stick for them, to get rid of them. Kelly went right for it, and Conrad was ready to grab the other end, but he stopped and sniffed the air. Suddenly he was gone, bounding across the field without a backward glance.

"The bitch in heat down the road," Mark said in a weary voice.

I went to collect Conrad in the car. The bitch was inside the house, but Conrad was throwing his body against the back door. The farmer's wife came out and together we got Conrad into my Volvo. "I thought Conrad was too young for this kind of thing," I said.

"How old is he?"

"Almost five months. He tries it with his sister, but I've been told it's more of a dominance thing."

"He's getting there. At least he has the instinct. But of all the times for Cindy to be in heat," she said sympathetically. "With the police dogs and all. I told Alf we're getting her done this time. He doesn't believe in tampering with nature. Have you people heard anything?"

I shook my head. With her round face she seemed like a motherly woman. If Mark and Emma had been other neighbours she would have been over with a casserole, I thought. But Mark had always kept his distance from the rural hoi-polloi.

"You tell the Richmans I'm here if they need anything."

I knew where I had to go now. I warned Conrad to behave and something in my voice told him I meant business. I felt light-headed, unreal, not sick as I had been yesterday, but as if I were back in one of the crazy dreams of last night. The sensible thing would have been to return to Mark and Emma's. They would worry if I didn't return, but there was something I had to do.

First things first. If I settled the one thing, I had the feeling that everything else would turn out all right.

Johnny's eyes were red when he answered the door. But not red from tears. I could smell that old, half-forgotten odour of pot, sweet and rich. It was something I hadn't smelled in years, not since the filmmaker forged one of my cheques for a hundred dollars and bought a bag. I wondered if Johnny had gotten it from Plymouth's friends.

I had left Conrad in the car because of Hans, but the German Shepherd was pretty mellow as well. And red-eyed, too, for that matter, I thought, as Johnny held the door open for me.

"Do you have any aerosol spray?"

Johnny looked at me: was I being the disapproving middle-aged lady?

"No really, I'm serious. There's someone else I want to hear what I have to say. And smelling the weed— well, let's not compromise the guy I'm about to invite over. I'm not that ancient, Johnny."

He didn't take his eyes off mine.

"I know who killed your father."

"There should be a can of spray upstairs."

I don't know what inspired me to call Neil Andersen. Maybe I was afraid I'd change my mind, or lose my nerve; or maybe I was just plain scared. Mark and Peter were both out of commission and probably I felt I just needed a witness, someone with common sense whom I could trust.

By the time Neil arrived, lilac fragrance spray and the aroma of good Melitta coffee had somewhat dispelled the smell of marijuana. Not that it mattered, I felt. Neil would have other matters to care about.

It was his day off, Neil informed us. He had been in Toronto, visiting with his daughter who was a student at the Ontario College of Art. He hadn't watched the news last night and the only newspaper he'd seen was *Now* at his daughter's apartment. He had no idea that Thomas and Matthew had been kidnapped.

Kidnapped. That was his word, after I summed up what had happened. Kidnapped. The realization made me telephone Mark and Emma's house to say I was safe. "Tell Mark I know what happened to Johnny's father," I instructed a mystified, disgruntled Hugh.

I waited until we all had our coffee before us. For a second, the kitchen seemed unreal, as did the faces before me. I hadn't had anything substantial to eat since Marion's breakfast, and suddenly I was very hungry. Could Johnny make me some toast? I asked.

Would they think I was silly? What if I was wrong? Neil looked tired, Johnny puzzled but patient.

"You think I'm nuts, with all that has happened with my nephew and my friend's son," I told Neil while Johnny buttered my toast.

Neil shrugged, and I saw him giving Johnny the barest glance:
Let's humour the lady. They watched while I gobbled down the toast.
Hans watched, too. I threw him a crust.

"This is a story. There was this mother and her son. Just the two
of them. No father. We don't know what happened to the father.
Perhaps he died in the war, or maybe he was married to someone
else. Anyway, a mother and her son. She brings him up as best she
can in a small village. But something is wrong. The son is different.
There are stories, maybe a little scandal. So the mother decides they
had better move somewhere else, and they come to Canada.

"The mother and son continued on together. They were nice
people and eventually bought some land in the country where they
could raise dogs. They were both dog lovers. From time to time
someone wondered why the son did not marry, but people attributed
this to his mother, who wanted him all for herself. They were wrong.
The mother would gladly have seen her son marry, because then this
shameful thing would not be true.

"So they went along. They didn't have a bad life. They had their
home, their beloved dogs. They made friends at card parties. Besides
this shameful secret, this thing, the mother was disappointed that her
son had not risen in the world. He was smart at school, practical but
not a scholar. Good at figuring things out. Mechanically inclined. He
worked here and there, getting jobs through the union hall and
sometimes working under the table. Over the years, though, work
had become scarcer and scarcer, and the mother worried. There was
probably still a mortgage on the farm, and their bit of savings would
not last long.

"Then this secure, steady job comes up at the School Board. This
would mean a decent and regular wage. And a pension. But this is a
School Board and school means children. The mother knows how
people think, how they will feel about her son working around kids.
She lies awake at night and worries. Who knows? Who knows about

her son? Who will tell? She has always kept at her son to keep this thing secret, but he likes the occasional drop of liquor and he has friends.

"At the same time, at the very same time that her son has applied for this position, a neighbour tells her she had better keep her son away from his boy. The neighbour knows about the job application, because his son has let this slip. The neighbour tells the mother that if she doesn't keep her son away from his son, he will ensure that her son never gets this position, as he's not fit to be around children.

"So she knows she has to prevent this from happening. She has no money, no real money, that she could use to bribe this man. And in any case, she's a frugal Scotswoman. So she knows she has to kill this neighbour.

"The only problem is his dog, his vicious German Shepherd dog. She has to wait until the man's son is away. At first the dog is the big problem because she hates the dog and is afraid of it, but then she realizes that the German Shepherd dog will help her. He will be the perfect shield. Her own dog, an older unspayed female, comes in heat. All she has to do is to take her dog there.

"Hans runs out before this man can stop him. Well, he can't stop him. She pulls out an old Luger, which her husband or father had brought back from Germany as a war trophy, and shoots this man who wants to ruin her son's name, reputation, future and well-being. After she shoots her enemy, she manages to leash her dog and— tie it to a tree. Or something. She doesn't have to try very hard to get Hans, now that he's through, back into the house. He's drawn there anyway, by the smell of blood. She shuts the door and walks her dog home. And there is the problem. As she is unlocking the door, her dog takes off. At first, she is too afraid to look for her dog, but you have to remember she is a great dog lover. She is worried her dog will be hit by a car. So, against her better judgement, she goes out looking for her dog. People see her looking, and offer to help. No one connects her to the shooting. She is just doing what any good dog owner would do.

"Later that night, while her son sleeps after drinking too much, she plants the gun in the van belonging to her enemy's son. She knows where he parks the van, she knows where he goes: to the den of iniquity where her own son has often been lured. It's not really her son's fault, you see. It is all the others who tempt him, and bring him to perversity."

I looked at Neil and Johnny, who looked back at me. All I could think, now, was that I was very hungry and that I wanted something else to eat.

"Except I'm not gay," Johnny said quietly.

"But your father was afraid you were. Or that you'd become gay, hanging around with undesirables like Plymouth. He was always after you to stop seeing Plymouth and his friends, wasn't he? He knew Scottie was gay and had seen you and Scottie together, maybe around Guelph. He was afraid Scottie would corrupt you, just as Mabel blamed you and your friends for corrupting her son. Scottie promised to take her on a holiday back to Scotland if he got the new job. Scottie told me and Peter that he planned to do this when we went to play cards there."

"Scottie is gay," Johnny admitted. "I've known for a long time. But it's no one's business but his. He never hurt anyone or anything. He's still in the closet. He never said, but I've always thought his mother didn't want anyone to know. And I don't think it bothers him that much, not coming out. He's always seemed pretty content to me. His dogs, his mother, playing cards, having a few drinks. He's had some friends. Lovers. A few people know in Guelph. I know his mother saw him with Plymouth once. A bunch of us were drinking beer and Scottie was supposed to meet her downtown after a doctor's appointment, but Scottie forgot, and she drove his old truck to the bar. She was sitting in it, waiting for him, when we came out. So she knew where he went drinking, and who with. Once he got in the truck, Scottie never looked back. I could see that she was giving him hell as they drove away."

"You wouldn't think she'd want to go back home where people knew," Neil said to me.

"She's getting old. They wouldn't have to go back to their home town. Or she wanted to show her old neighbours that Scottie had reformed. Maybe she just longed for the old country. All this secrecy! If people had known about Scottie and accepted him, there would not have been a problem. Do you have any eggs or anything, Johnny? I am just absolutely famished."

"You're dreaming if you think it's all easy street if everything's in the open," Johnny said. "Maybe you're right about Mabel, but she was right, too. I bet if the powers that be knew about Scottie, they wouldn't hire him." He opened the fridge.

"How did you put all this together?" Neil asked.

"It just came to me. Dogs in heat. Gays. Scottie's job prospects." I shook my head. I could not really describe that moment of knowing, when it had all seemed simple. "And I thought of Scottie giving me a lift home one night when I had Conrad out for a walk downtown. Scottie had been driving around, he said, after a card game. He'd been drinking and I could smell whiskey. But there was something else. An odour of after-shave, which I'd never smelled on Scottie before. I doubted if it was his."

I looked at the clock on the wall. It was almost five. Thomas and Matthew.

"Except for breakfast, I've hardly eaten since we had 'lunch' at Mabel's almost forty-eight hours ago," I explained to Neil as Johnny rummaged in the fridge. "And I think she tried to poison me. Arsenic in the egg sandwiches, probably."

Neil raised an eyebrow.

Chapter Eighteen

Neil made a phone call before we left and learned that Matthew and Thomas had been found safe and sound near North Bay at just about the time I looked at the clock.

He drove me back to Mark and Emma's. I was suddenly— suddenly?— it seemed as though I had been exhausted, wobbly, spent, through the wringer, whatever, for days and days— finished. I knew as soon as I got behind the wheel of my car that I could not drive. "Move over," Neil said gruffly, and I gladly slid over into the passenger seat.

We didn't speak. Even Conrad was quiet. I was still hungry.

Peter was waiting for me. Whatever irritation Peter— and the others— felt about my indecorous, untimely flight— was gone by the time Neil drove our Volvo into the driveway. The boys were safe; that was all that mattered.

Jensen, being from Minnesota, had chosen to drive home by the northern route, through Ontario along Lake Superior. He and his wife had abandoned the rental car north of Toronto near Barrie, picked up their van, and headed for Sault Ste. Marie. It was only later that we learned that it was Matthew's idea for both boys to give false names. Thomas, Matthew told me later, began crying and wanted to obey these strange people, but Matthew did his best to keep him calm. Maybe the fact that Jensen was heading in the direction of Meredith gave Matthew courage.

Jensen and his wife argued, Matthew said. Jensen said only one boy could be his son, but the wife ("Betty") said that God had given them two boys and they should be happy. She had even packed a picnic lunch, Matthew told us, but the tuna sandwiches were yucky: too much mayonnaise. And they pulled off the road when it started to get dark because the lights on the van weren't working, which accounted for the passage of time. A flat tire delayed them further.

Jensen and Betty made the boys change into girls' clothing, including pink toques, but it was Matthew's luck that Jensen stopped at Harper's Esso, just the other side of Meredith. The owner was an old friend of Joe's who'd known Matthew since he was in diapers. Matthew knew he was home free as soon as Jensen rolled down the window to pay for the fill-up. It was all over Meredith, of course, that Matthew had been kidnapped.

Pierre, the owner of Harper's Esso, simply removed the distributor cap wire when he checked the oil of the van.

Perhaps I was a coward for not confronting Mabel directly. I wondered if she'd tried to poison me. I prefer to think not. Maybe I'd only caught Emma's flu. If Mabel'd had any motive at all to hurt me, it was after Scottie blathered about his job prospects, but by then the sandwiches, pickles and pie had gone down the hatch. Besides, Peter had heard, too, and he hadn't become ill.

In any case, I'm glad I wasn't there when Mabel cracked. Maybe my cowardice had as much to do with sorrow and regret as concern for my personal safety. Seeing that proud, proud woman reduced to tears was not a prospect I welcomed. According to Mark, Mabel finally confessed when confronted with her son's homosexuality, though she denied this to the end. People telling such lies about Humphrey, accusing her son of perversion, excused the murder, she insisted. I can imagine her crying, "I will never believe it, never, never!" Pounding the table, as tears ran down her face. I picture her wearing her tweed coat, reaching into the pocket for an old linen handkerchief...

I have to say that Mark was disappointed the murder of George Austin-Wright had nothing to do with the Romanovs and the legend of Anastasia. He was left with a free client, but a lot of loose ends. It was pointless, he admitted, to pursue seeing the "Anastasia" letters in Johnny's mother's possession, but I know for a fact that Marion, on Mark's behalf, made another approach to Marlies Van Simp. An unsuccessful approach. The letters and papers and whatever secrets they contain remain with Marlies.

Emma and Mark are still together, but going for counselling. I'd like to be able to say that Thomas' safe return cemented their relationship, but after the relief had passed, Emma was still talking about returning to Holland.

Allison drove back to Meredith with Joe, who finally surfaced from the bush the day after Matthew's safe return. I miss Matthew like crazy, and sometimes I actually wish Allison would head south again. But Allison's been accepted for nurse's training in North Bay for next year, and even if things don't work out with Joe, she'll probably stick to northern Ontario for a while.

Plymouth's murderer was never caught and the case is still on the books. But I wonder. The lights in that house were turned off and I picture frugal, thrifty Mabel automatically turning off the lights, just as she turned off her living room lights when we went to the kitchen for lunch. If she had known that Plymouth was coming for dinner at my place, that would also have been a reason to poison me. Plymouth knew about Scottie; Plymouth knew me; I knew Mark, and Mark was on the School Board hiring committee. But as often as I picture Mabel's china cups, the teapot, the hen-shaped butter dish, I can find no evidence, no suspicious acts on her part.

I learned from Mark that in jail, Mabel kept crying, "What will happen to Humphrey if I'm not there? What will he do without me?" She'd gone on and on about having to assure her son's future when she was gone, and hinted that she was dying.

A medical examination in prison revealed that Mabel was suffering from a long-standing bladder infection. She had visited a doctor regularly for her arthritis, but the symptoms of the bladder condition had been too embarrassing for Mabel to mention. She might have been afraid, I thought, that she had caught something from Scottie through meals or doing his laundry. The infection grew worse and worse, and Mabel suspected she had cancer. Securing Scottie's future was paramount. He would never survive without her. More secrecy. More unnecessary secrecy...

Poor Scottie had no idea, none at all, of what his mother had done. With Mabel "away," the last thing he wanted was a full-time job. There were the dogs to consider, and he would never take a trip to Scotland alone...

"Even if nothing that happened was related to the Romanovs, I thought you'd like to have this."

Peter was in a great mood. He'd fired Muriel. Well, not exactly fired her. Mark needed a file clerk in his office, and Peter knew of the perfect candidate...

"I could have saved this for Christmas, but what the hell! You can see why the lumpen proletariat rebelled, but they sure knew how to live, the Romanovs!"

The book he gave me was *Tsar: The Lost World of Nicholas and Alexandra*, by Peter Kurth, who had previously written a biography of Anna Anderson, whom he sincerely believed to be Anastasia.

It was a heavy, coffee table book, glossy and sumptuous. I turned pages looking at palaces, parks, Fabergé eggs, paintings, golden pillars and lofty staircases. There were pictures of the Alexander Palace at Tsarskoe Selo, the Tsar's village, which Anna Anderson had talked about. She had also talked about Livadia, the Tsar's estate in the Crimea, where, she said, there had been a wonderful birdhouse filled with exotic species.

And mingled with these elegant pictures, overwhelming in their richness, were photos the family had taken themselves, pictures of the

Tsarina's famous mauve boudoir, pictures of the girls kneeling by Alexandra's bedside, pictures of the little Tsarevich in his sailor suit, pictures of the family picnicking in the Finnish countryside, where they had gone ashore while on a cruise on their fabulous yacht, *The Standart*.

And pictures, too, of the family in captivity. A wan Tsarevich held up thin hands to the camera. The young Grand Duchesses, wearing caps because their hair had been shaved after they had measles, sunned themselves. Alexandra sat in a wheelchair...

And pictures of bones, when it was all over, after the slaughter in the basement of the house in Ekaterinburg, their final prison.

Anna Anderson was there in the book, too. The first pictures taken of her shortly after she was rescued from the canal in Berlin in 1920 showed a young woman who did not, in the least, resemble Anastasia. Anna/Franziska gave a half-smile for the camera, a mocking, mischievous smile: I will fool you. You don't know who I am at all...

"It's wonderful," I told Peter, who was opening a bottle of wine to celebrate Muriel's departure.

"Thought you'd like it."

"We'll have to give your mother a copy for Christmas," I said.

"The idea did occur to me."

He passed me my wine and I moved the book over, so as not to spill anything on it. And I wanted to save it, to look at alone, later. I knew that the palace photos would pall, that all that richness would be too much, like cloying cake, and that I would turn to the part about Franziska over and over again.

How had she done it? Had someone from Russia helped her, perhaps showing her these very pictures, some of them hidden in archives? And had she believed in herself as Anastasia? I wondered, opening the book quickly to look at her as an old woman, a real crone. I closed the book again and wondered what I would tell Marlies if one day the phone rang and she said she had vastly reduced the price of her "documents."

"Good-bye, Muriel!" Peter raised his glass in a toast. "Good riddance, you old bat."

He hugged me. Conrad nudged between us, spilling my wine on the carpet.

"Lick, lick," Peter instructed, sticking out his tongue to demonstrate.

But Conrad wanted no part of the red wine. We had finally found a substance Conrad wouldn't beg, borrow, or steal.